Breaking
Ryann

Breaking Ryann

BAD BOY REFORMED SERIES BOOK THREE

usa today bestselling author
alyssa rae taylor

Copyright © 2015 by Alyssa Rae Taylor LLC.
All Rights Reserved.

This is a work of fiction. Except for the work created by the imagination of the author, all names, places, songs and song titles are the property of their trademark owners. The use of these trademarks in the publication is not authorized, associated or sponsored by their trademark owners.

Cover art by Sarah Hansen/Okay Creations.
Copyediting by Madison Seidler (madisonseidler.com)
Interior design and formatting by

E.M. TIPPETTS BOOK DESIGNS

www.emtippettsbookdesigns.com

books by
alyssa rae taylor

Bad Boy Reformed Series
Raising Ryann
Resisting Ryann
Breaking Ryann

Chapter

REESE

One

"Keep doing that," Sean breathes, pulling my bottom lip into his mouth before releasing it.

I scratch my nails up and down his back, running my other hand through his golden brown hair. He's got it cut really short, and I like it. "This?"

He switches to my top lip. "Yeah, it feels good," he says, hungrily moving back and forth over my mouth. When he rocks against me, our tongues collide. I softly moan, enjoying the friction it brings. He squeezes my breast then glides down my quivering stomach, meeting the edge of my shorts. The familiar confusion settles in.

"Are you wet for me?" His voice is husky as his fingers slip inside of my panties. Desire pools in his eyes.

It's all in your head, Reese. You can do this.

Meeting his gaze, he asks, "Do you want me?"

I feel conflicted, not wanting to hurt him. He senses my hesitation and rolls off me, rubbing the space between his brows.

"It still feels like we're rushing things. I'm sorry."

"Don't worry," he replies, clearly frustrated. "Give me a minute to lose this semi, and I'll be fine."

"I didn't mean to get your hopes up." I scoot back against the headboard and fasten my shorts. He lets out an exaggerated breath. It's been a few months since we've called our relationship 'official.' He's never pressured me for sex, but it's clear my hesitancy is wearing on him.

"It's your first time. You're nervous," he replies, looking straight ahead. I can tell he's thinking into it. Ever since Luke's return, I've sensed his insecurity. We haven't spoken since the night he came back, but it doesn't make Sean feel any better. He knows how much Luke meant to me.

"You're leaving?" I ask as he climbs out of bed.

Grabbing his light blue polo, he pulls it over his head, and makes a weak attempt to cover his erection. "It's late," he says, tapping twice on the doorframe. "I should go." He starts down the hall.

"Wait." I jump out of bed, meeting him in the middle. "I love you. You know that, right?" We've said it before, but I want him to know that I mean it. "I'm just protecting my heart."

His eyes soften. I hope that means he believes me.

"What's up guys?" Logan calls from the other room.

We glance toward the couch, where he and Gia are spooning, the volume on the television set low. I purse my lips, unaware we had an audience, then my eyes move to the fresh bouquet of Calla lilies displayed on our table. A shot of fear bolts through me, and I try to speed things along, lightly pushing Sean forward. "Will I see you tomorrow, or will you be working?"

"Depends on what I get done tonight."

"Well, you better get going then."

"I'm goin'."

I move him to the door, and he pauses and turns to Logan.

"Dude. You're going to have to quit that." He tips his head toward the flowers with a half grin on his face. "You're making me look bad."

I cringe, glancing at Logan. To say he looks confused is an understatement.

"The flowers," Sean confirms.

Logan lifts his head. His eyes flick from me to the lilies before he relaxes against the pillow. He focuses back on the television. "Wish I could take the credit, man, but those aren't from me."

Gia silently apologizes with her eyes. Logan doesn't know any better. It isn't her fault. I'm the one who chose to lie to my boyfriend. Hurrying us out the door, I prepare for an argument.

"You lied to me," Sean says sharply, not wasting any time. His hair glistens under the porch light.

"It's not what you think."

"It's not? Because I'm thinking Luke sent you those flowers."

"You're right. He *did*," I pause, sighing. "But they don't mean anything. I just wasn't sure how to tell you. I knew it would upset you."

He looks disgusted. "And that makes it okay?"

I sit on the porch bench right outside the door. "Of course it doesn't. I should have been honest with you. Lying was stupid." Feeling defeated, I put my head in my hands.

"Is there anything else I need to know, while we're being honest with each other? Just get it all out now. I don't want any more surprises."

Uh yeah, Luke has a wife. I shake my head. "There's nothing." His jaw ticks like he doesn't believe me. "Stop reading into this like it's more than it is. They're just flowers, Sean."

"Just flowers," he murmurs lowly, rubbing his hand against

his forehead. "Is he the reason you won't let me fuck you?"

"Excuse me?" My stomach drops.

"You heard me."

"Of course not!" I stand and look directly into his eyes. I've always known this was in the back of his mind, but the way he said it hurts. "I can't believe you just said that!" Luke's dog barks across the way, and my gaze slides towards his place. "Keep your voice down! You're being loud."

"So what if he hears me," he spits.

"I told you. We haven't spoken since the day he moved back."

"How do I know that isn't bullshit?"

"Because it isn't." He only knows a quarter of what happened that night. I left out the candlelit dinner and the wife—a wife I've rarely seen around here. I assume they're having problems already. It wouldn't surprise me in the least.

Two days after we'd met on the rooftop, my heart shattered all over again, when I spotted a woman carrying boxes into his house. I recognized her immediately and ran to the toilet to dry heave, then silently bawled for an hour. I wasn't prepared to have it shoved in my face. A part of me had hoped that, if I let Luke explain like he'd asked, we'd somehow be able to move on from this, but my logical side told me to let him go. I didn't want to make the same mistakes as my mother—constantly living in denial. I refused to be *that* girl.

The next night I walked out my front door and came face to face with a large German Shepard. Startled, I took a cautious step back. He sat on his hind legs, lifting a paw like he wanted to shake. Hesitantly, I leaned down to pet him, admiring his brindle fur coat. *"Hey there, big boy. You scared me for a minute."* I smiled, and he happily panted in return. *"Good thing you're friendly. Are you lost?"*

"Chance," called the voice of the woman from the day before, standing in front of Luke's place. I froze when she walked over, sizing me up with an eyebrow raised. I'm not sure if she recognized me from the hospital. "I'm Rachelle," she said, reaching out her hand. It took me a second to take it. She exuded confidence and was disgustingly fit. I wanted to throw up again.

"Reese," I replied with a clear of my throat, before we shook hands.

Flipping her hair over her shoulder, her eyes fell on Chance. "Sorry. Blame it on his father. I told him Chance had mastered opening doors." She tipped her head toward *their* house. "But Luke had other things on his mind, if you know what I mean." She laughed half-heartedly. "You know men. Maybe next time he'll put him away first, like I'd asked." Reaching for his collar, she said, "C'mon boy. Let's go," dragging him back to the house. "It was nice to meet you," she said right as she shut the door.

That was the last time I saw her.

"For two damn months this has gone on! You couldn't tell him to stop?" Sean yells, snapping me out of the memory.

"I didn't want to face him. I … I thought if I ignored it, he'd get the hint and stop sending the flowers."

"You've got 'em in the center of your living room!"

"At first I threw them away, even using *his* garbage can, so he'd see them."

"You're giving him the wrong idea, Reese!"

"Stop yelling! I can hear you!" I shout, as loud as him.

"Are you going to tell him, or am I?" His fists clench at his sides.

"You okay, Reese?" Luke calls, standing twenty feet away. My breath catches as he strides over. Sean pulls me in for a possessive kiss, making things more awkward than they already are. Forcing my eyes shut, I give in, though I'm not done being pissed. What he'd said earlier was disrespectful, but I need to show him there's no reason for his insecurity. Luke and I are truly over.

"You gonna let her answer, or are we gonna stand here all night?"

My skin responds to the familiar voice as if it were touching me. *Oh God, he's so close.*

Sean releases me, wiping his mouth. "Mind your own business. She's not your concern anymore."

Ignoring Sean completely, Luke asks me again, "You okay Reese?" His eyes search deep, like he's invading my soul. Chills shoot up the back of my neck. I don't know how he does it. He's shirtless and freshly showered—wearing low-slung shorts that show off his muscular physique, and the sexy V framing his pelvic area, one I've been known to stare at.

I drag my eyes away from his body, breathing in his intoxicating scent. *He's married, Reese. He's a liar! Remember?*

"She'll be fine once you leave her alone. And stop sending the flowers," Sean growls. "She doesn't want them."

"You gonna buy them for her?" Luke asks without casting him a glance. A conflict of emotions burns inside my chest. *How can he be so protective on one hand, yet so hurtful on another?*

"I said she doesn't want you here, man. Go back inside."

The tension continues to thicken. I place a hand over Sean's chest, giving it a slight shove. "Let's get you home." *If he doesn't shut up, he's going to get his butt kicked.*

"Do you always let him speak for you?"

Whipping around to face Luke, I spit, "I think you know me better than that, and frankly, it's none of your business."

He moves a little too close, dipping down to meet my eyes. "You being honest with me?"

Then Sean's up in Luke's face. "She can't stand being near you, asshole! Take the fucking hint!"

Luke smirks, taunting him. "You keep telling yourself that, buddy. Reese and I have a past. I can read her like a book." He straightens his shoulders. "Whether she's hiding something, her emotions, her truths, her lies ... all of it."

Oh God ... where is he going with this?

"That's special. Really, I'm touched. But where were you when her father died, huh? 'Cause I was drying her tears, picking up the pieces you left behind. You dumb piece of shit!"

I watch Luke's expression change to lethal. When he turns to me, his jaw is clenched. "If you care about him at all, you'll convince him to walk away." His voice is a low growl.

I take his threat seriously, grabbing onto Sean's arm. "It's late. You have work to do. Remember?" I plead, keeping my voice as calm as I can muster, but I'm not sure that it's helping. He still hasn't budged.

"Tell him what you said about the flowers. I'll go home once you're inside. I'd be crazy to leave him alone with you."

"Luke would never hurt me."

He snorts, then Luke rams himself hard into his chest. "Something funny, prick?" Before I can blink, he's bumping him again. There isn't a contest on who would win, if things got ugly. Luke's an expert, and he towers over Sean.

I work my way between them, placing a hand on both of their chests, giving Sean a look of warning. Then I turn my attention to Luke. "I don't think it's appropriate that you send me flowers." A lump forms in my throat. "I need you to stop." *Why do I feel sorry for him?*

His hands slip deep into his pockets, and slowly he backs away, showing no flicker of emotion. "Done," is all he says.

I lift my chin. *Glad I've made it easy. Now run along to your wife, wherever she is.*

When he reaches his front door, I give Sean a glare. He's still on my shit list. "Told you—you have nothing to worry about."

He wraps his arms around me, kissing the side of my neck, even though I slightly protest. "Something tells me he's not done yet."

"You'll see."

"That's what I'm afraid of."

"See you in the morning," Luke calls from his doorway. His arms stretched out wide, he grips the frame.

Sean tenses, and I stare at Luke, confused.

"The morning?"

Every ripple of his torso is on display under the porch light. "Work," he replies, with his gaze fixed on Sean, no matter that I'm who asked the question. "I'm back at the gym."

My mouth falls open, the beat of my heart triples its pace, and I stand there, speechless.

Chapter

REESE

Two

The moment I arrive at work, my eyes land on Luke's Chevy parked at the far end of the parking lot. Not that I hadn't expected it to be there, but seeing it drove home that we'd be working together again. His words kept me up all night, but I eventually came to the conclusion that it was time to put on my big girl panties and deal with this like an adult. So that's what I plan to do.

I make a beeline for the entrance, hoping Luke isn't near the front. The windows are tinted, and it's hard to see who's standing there. *Big girl panties*, I remind myself. My eyes connect with Pam's as soon as I push through the door. She greets me from behind the counter, and as she does, I wonder why she hadn't warned me about his coming back? Does she know anything about her foster son, or has he been feeding her lies as well?

"Hello there, beautiful." Pam smiles in a perkier mood than normal, though I've rarely seen her unhappy.

"You're extra cheerful this morning." I shove my purse behind the counter before reaching to give her a hug.

She pulls back and rests her hands on my shoulders. "Luke is here with one of your students who was dropped off a little early. He told me you were aware of his coming back?" Concerned, her brows bunch together. "This isn't going to be a problem for you, is it?"

"Why would it be? I was a little surprised by the short notice, but other than that, I don't see it being a problem." I shrug, hoping I sounded convincing.

"I'm sorry. It wasn't until last night that he gave a definitive answer. Jim and I are thrilled. We've missed him." Her eyes light up.

"I bet," I reply, wondering if she knows about the wife. A pang of jealousy comes over me, and I mentally squash it, reminding myself of his lies. "Guess I should get to work then."

She gives her two thumbs up without looking suspicious of my fake chipper attitude. "Good luck today!"

I smile in return. *Thanks. I'm going to need it.* Looking out over the gym, I'm surprised it's so quiet. The weekends are usually crowded with the additional teenagers who are out of school. I peek at my reflection in the mirrors along the way—happy with how my skin glows.

I worked on my appearance, making my green eyes pop. Is it wrong that I want Luke to mourn what he's lost? To realize he made a mistake?

Once I reach my destination, he's sitting next to my student inside the cage. I recognize the long blond hair to be Erica's. *Good luck getting her to talk*, I think, stepping inside. My breath catches when I notice the smile on her heart-shaped face. *How'd he do it?* My palm lies over my burning chest. Even eye contact with Erica has always been a struggle for me. Earning a smile's like winning the lottery.

"Hey there!" I give her my best grin.

Her blue eyes take me in. I don't expect that she'll say anything, and she doesn't.

Spotting the color on her cheeks, I tip my head toward the culprit. "I see you've already met Luke."

"Yep." She nods, as we both stretch out on the floor.

"Good. He'll be helping out with our class." I grab my feet and bring my forehead to my knees. *Ugh ... how am I going to work like this?* He's staring, and it's incredibly uncomfortable. I think I feel my face twitching. *Awesome.*

After half the kids arrive, I make the decision to talk to him. This isn't going to work if I ignore him the whole time. "Girls, can you excuse us for a moment?" I motion for Luke to follow me, then make my way to the break room. When I turn around, he slams right into me, unprepared for my sudden stop. "Whoa." My hands land on his chest. It's as though electricity jolts straight through me.

"Sorry." He backs up with a clear of his throat. Very slowly, his eyes travel over me. I don't want to welcome the heat it brings me. His fingers twitch like wants to touch me, but he holds back, straightening his shoulders. His hair is a little longer, and his chiseled jaw is lightly shadowed in stubble. He looks even more handsome than I remember.

"We need to talk," I tell him.

"It's been awhile since I've seen you in the daylight. You look good." He swallows, meeting my eyes. "Are you happy?" The question seems genuine, like he *really* wants to know.

"I know what you're doing. It isn't going to work this time."

His forehead creases. "What is it you think I'm doing exactly?"

Oh please. You know what you're doing. "Trying to make me feel sorry for you. I'm smarter than you think, Luke."

"Well shit. I guess you've figured me out then." He tugs on his hair. "Look, I'm sorry if—"

"Are you? Are you *really*?" *Of course he's not sorry. If he were sorry, he would've left me alone like he'd told me he would.*

"I said it. Didn't I?" He frowns, looking around the empty break room then back to me.

"You say a lot of things you don't mean."

"All right, I deserve that." He drops his head and continues, "But when are you gonna to give me a chance to talk? There are things I need to say—things I've wanted to say for a long time."

"Oh no. You fooled me once. I'm not going to let you do it again." I shake my head. "You and I've got no relationship outside this gym." A sick feeling stirs inside my belly, as soon as the words leave my mouth. The love and hatred I feel for this man only brings me confusion. Why can't it be just one or the other?

"There's no reason we can't be friends, Reese. You're good for me," he murmurs.

"Huh, well you're not good for me. And there are several reasons why we can't be friends." *Who is he kidding?*

He steps toward me with narrowed eyes, and his clean soapy scent washes over me. "Why won't you let me explain? What are you afraid of?"

I notice the way his shirt stretches over his muscled chest, and how his arms flex against his sleeves. "I'm not afraid of anything."

"Yeah." His voice is soft as he moves closer; his brown eyes reel me in. "Well I think you're lying."

Don't fall for his charm, Reese. I back away and find my voice. "I don't care what you think. We keep things professional. Are we clear?"

He rubs a palm over his face, then with an exaggerated breath, he agrees, "Yes ma'am. Crystal."

"Will you be able to control your urges?"

Blinking three times before he cups a hand behind his ear, he says, "My what?"

He knows what I said.

"Could you repeat that? I don't think I heard you right." His mouth twitches.

I'm not trying to be funny. "Your urges," I growl. "The flirty comments, the sexual innuendoes, and inappropriate touching. Can you keep a handle on that?"

"I was getting ready to ask you the same thing." He leans back, folding his arms.

"And that thing you're doing with your eyes. You definitely can't do that."

"My eyes?" He laughs incredulously. "What the hell are you talking about?" he asks, placing his palm over my forehead. "You feeling okay?"

I'm mad this entertains him. "You're breaking a rule right now!"

"I asked you a question!"

"You were smirking, the way you do, where just the left dimple shows. You do that when you're flirting!" My eyes land on his dimple. *And I can't control how I feel when you do those things.*

I can tell this pinches a nerve with him. "Your rules are impossible. What if I don't agree to them?"

"If you respect me, you will! End of story!"

"Fine! We done?"

"Yes!" I say in response, but he doesn't hear me. He's already left the room.

Chapter
REESE
Three

Despite our confrontation, class moves along swiftly. Luke and the girls connect right off the bat, which isn't a surprise. He's a natural. When I encouraged him to take over the rest of the period, it was clear I'd shocked him. Guess he doesn't know me like he says he does. To be honest, I wasn't ready to teach, knowing he'd be watching. Relationship aside, I've seen him work with the kids, and I enjoy their interaction.

"You ready, Reese?"

"Huh?" I'm quickly snapped out of my thoughts.

He takes a quick peek at the clock. "We've got ten minutes. You want to help me demonstrate, or is it breaking one of your rules?"

His snide remark doesn't get past me. It's obvious his ego's been bruised. "You mean you and me?" I stand up. *Of course he means us! And why did my voice just squeak?*

"Yes." A hint of a smirk plays on his lips as he nods slowly. "Do you think you can you handle that?" he says, throwing my words back at me.

I lift my chin and tug on the hem of my shorts. "Can you?" Okay, so maybe I'm bluffing, 'cause I have no idea what we're demonstrating. My mind just sort of drifted off for a bit.

"Ooohhh," some of the girls say out loud. They're lined up with their backs against the cage.

"This is going to be good," Taylor says on the end, while the rest of them snicker with one another.

"What? You don't think I can take him?"

Luke's eyes connect with mine. "I don't know. She's pretty tough."

"But you're stronger," Maddy replies.

Figures they'd take his side.

"You want to back out?" he asks, looking all too smug.

I raise an arched brow. "Now why in the world would I do that?"

He gives a single nod. "Okay then." Turning toward the girls, he adds, "I'm gonna take her down and attempt to choke her." He's got their undivided attention. "Watch us carefully. It may save your life one day." Switching his gaze back to me, he asks, "You ready?"

Yeah, now that you've just explained.

I give him the go ahead, and he comes at me, easily taking me down so that I'm flat on my back. Pressing my palms against his chest as he straddles me, I can feel his steady heartbeat. His large hands wrap around my throat, squeezing with light pressure. We stare into one another's eyes, and I lose my concentration, getting sucked in.

"You okay?" he whispers, scanning my face with concern.

Keeping my elbows close to my body, I place my folded arms over his. "I'm fine," I grit out, pressing down on his forearms. *Why does he have to look at me like that?* I groan inwardly. Flashes of our tangled limbs and tongues begin to fill my brain, then the sexual promises he'd once made me ... a rush of warmth pools between my legs. *What the hell? Is it really that easy for him?*

I lift my hips as high as they can go, keeping my arms in the same position. When I slam them to the ground, I do a crunch at the same time, bending his arms. This loosens his grip enough so that I can place my feet above his knees, pushing down on his thighs. He grunts, and I scoot away, forcing him to release me. "That's enough for today," I pant, feeling my chest rise and fall. "Class is over." Standing up, I put my hands on my hips unable to look at him. I'm embarrassed. *God, I hope he didn't notice. There are children around, for heaven's sake, yet he still manages to arouse me.*

"We'll go over this again next week," I hear Luke say from behind me.

The girls pile out of the cage. I follow the line to escape the awkwardness. *C'mon, girls. Move along.*

"What happened back there?"

I stay where I am. There's *no way* I'm giving him the truth. "I guess I'm a little rusty." Turning around, I add, "It's been awhile since somebody's tried to choke me."

His eyes roam over me like he's trying to figure me out. "Were you afraid?"

I can tell he actually believes this. Why? I don't know. "Don't give yourself too much credit. You don't scare me."

The cords in his tattooed arm flex as he grips the back of his neck. "Do you want me to quit?"

"What if I said yes?"

He strides toward me, stopping just a few inches away. "Then I'll go."

"It's not up to me."

"You and I both know it is."

I swallow, and he watches the movement.

"Pam would hate me."

He shrugs. "I'll make up an excuse."

"You'd really leave the gym for me?" I look at him, skeptical.

He nods once. "If that's what you wanted."

"It isn't." The words come out fast. "You're good with them. I don't have to tell you that. They like you, and you leaving wouldn't be fair to them." I convince myself that this is the only reason he should stay.

Those cognac-colored eyes take me in. It's hard not to fidget, but I can't look away. "You sure that's what you want?"

"Yeah."

A slow grin spreads across his face. "Then I'll stay."

"Don't get any ideas." I blow a strand of hair that falls out of place, and he gently tucks it away, making my skin prickle. His eyes move from my neck, down my arms. "Look, I don't know what's going on in your … personal life," I clear my throat, "but I mean it, Luke. I'm not that kind of girl."

He frowns. "You think I don't know what kind of girl you are?"

"I'm not sure what to think anymore."

"Where is this coming from? The preppy douche bag living in my house?"

"Don't bring him into this. He's got a name."

"And you were quick to find out what it is. Weren't you?" he snarls.

"That's hardly fair. Don't you think?"

He tugs on his already messy hair. "Fuck fair! Nothing about us has been fair!"

My eyes widen, glancing around to see if anyone is watching. There are people in the other room, but far enough away that they probably didn't hear him. When I turn back, I narrow my eyes. "You did this! You brought this upon yourself!" I hiss. "Remember?" *You ran off and married someone else!* Knowing my voice will probably crack, I don't say that part out loud, but I can feel it fighting to burst out of me.

"I can't stand him putting his *tiny* hands on you. He's lucky he's still breathing after the show he put on last night."

"I didn't mean for you to see that. I'm sorry." I wouldn't want him sucking face with his wife in my presence. It was bad enough hearing her go on about their sex life the way that she did.

"Do you love him?"

My brows rise to my hairline. He has a lot of nerve asking me that. "This conversation is officially over." I start walking away, saying over my shoulder, "You of all people shouldn't be asking me that."

"It's a simple yes or no answer," he replies from behind me.

I scurry off to put some distance between us, my head down so no one will try to talk to me. I send Gia a text, needing my best friend. I just hope she'll be able to forgive me when I finally tell her what I've been hiding.

Chapter

REESE

Four

"You're sure you're not on medication ... something that could bring on delusions?" Gia stands in her pajamas, pouring herself another glass of wine. I'd just informed her about Luke having a wife, as well as the night he'd surprised me on the rooftop. I should have known she would react this way. I guess I thought she'd take my word for it.

I roll my eyes. "I'm not crazy. She's real."

"I don't think you're crazy." She bites her lip. "But if this is true, it would mean Logan's been lying all this time."

"Not necessarily. What if he doesn't know?" It wasn't my intention to get Logan in trouble.

"Are you kidding? Logan would definitely know."

"Maybe," I murmur, quickly picking a piece of lint from my pants. "But what if he doesn't?"

"I don't think Luke would keep something like that from him. It's too big of a deal." She rests her chin in her hand. "Maybe it's all a misunderstanding. That would make more sense." Tilting her head, she continues, "Think about it. We would have seen her around by now."

"I've seen her." I play with the stem of my glass. "I've seen her a couple of times."

Twisting a curl around her finger, her brows bunch together. "Outside of the hospital?"

"Yeah." I move to the couch. Gia follows and plops down next me. "She was carrying boxes into their house," I continue. "The next time their dog had gotten out. She came over to collect him and introduced herself."

We sit in silence for a moment, before she asks the dreaded question. "What does she look like?"

I groan, remembering her confidence, the sway of her silky dark hair, and nicely toned body. "Like she belongs on the cover of *Cosmo*."

"You've always been an exaggerator." She playfully nudges me. "I bet she doesn't compare to you."

"Thanks, but it's true." I inhale a long, slow breath, before quickly releasing it, "Anyway, it shouldn't matter. I've moved on."

"Have you?" Her face is sympathetic. "You don't seem very happy. You haven't for a long time."

Has it seemed that way to everyone? I close my eyes. "Aside from being confused, I don't know what I am anymore."

"Let's go over some details again." She folds her legs, getting comfy. "It'll help me process."

"Okay."

"You're at the hospital talking with one of the nurses." She lifts her brows to confirm.

"Correct."

"Then a woman comes in and asks for Luke Ryann's room."

I lick my lips, laying my head against the couch. "At first I thought I was hearing things, but then it made sense since I'd seen his sister there earlier. It never really crossed my mind she'd been there for Luke ... until that moment."

"Plus, you thought Luke was thousands of miles away at the time. Must have been pretty shocking."

"To say the least." I give a defeated laugh. "I wanted to see him—find out what had happened, and if he was okay. That's when a nurse walked up and recognized the woman, saying she was his wife. She said she had been there twice." I cringe at the memory.

"What happened next?"

"I watched as she led her to his room. The rest is all a blur."

"And you never found out why he was there?" she asks softly.

"I didn't get a chance ... but he obviously pulled through." I tip my head toward his house, finishing the rest of my wine.

She pours me another. "I need to talk to Logan," she says, topping off her own glass.

"Don't! I'd rather he not know. Luke's been hiding it for a reason, and telling you is humiliating enough."

"You're protecting him?"

I shake my head. "I'm protecting myself."

"You're so certain he doesn't know." She frowns. "What if you're wrong?"

"Logan's heart happens to belong to my best friend. Luke's probably not proud of the fact we were still together when it happened. He knows it was a dick move."

She nods, finally getting it. "So you're saying he doesn't want to look like a cheating bastard."

"Maybe he wants to play it off like they married after we split."

She twists a curl around her finger. "When was the last time you saw her?"

"It's been a couple months."

"Months?" Her brows bunch together. "Well, that's odd. Don't you think?"

"Maybe they're having problems?" I shrug. It's the only reason I can come up with. "Still doesn't change what he did."

Her eyes get huge. "Oh my God! I just thought of something! You know how you've been getting that feeling like someone's following you?"

"Yeah."

For the past month, I've seen the same white pickup truck show up in places I happen to be. I'd only noticed it because of the tin foil on the back passenger windows, and the bumper loaded with stickers. One time, late at night, I was driving on the other side of town. The roads weren't very busy, but I'd seen the same truck in my rearview, speeding up behind me. Right as a panic started to settle deep in my gut, the truck had passed me, cutting me off, before turning down a side street.

When I came home and explained it all to Gia, she'd blamed it on me watching too many scary movies. I'd figured she'd probably been right, and haven't had a run in with it since.

"What if it's her? What if they're having problems because she found out about you, and now she's stalking you?" She bubbles up in laughter.

"I don't think that's funny."

"Well, what if it's her?"

"The truck had tin foil all over the back windows and a crap load of bumper stickers — not exactly a vehicle I'd place her in."

"True." She taps her finger over her lips. "Back to that night on the rooftop ... the rose petals, the gifts, the set up with the candles, the dinner ... why would he do that?"

"I don't know. To apologize, I guess."

"And you said he admitted it? Told you he got married?"

"Not in those words, but yes." I take another drink. The liquid burns going down. So I pound a fist against my chest, and my eyes water.

"You never told me his explanation."

"That's because you called me delusional."

"Sorry," she replies gently.

I sigh. "He apologized. Said he hoped I'd find it in my heart to forgive him. It seemed sincere enough. He was genuinely upset."

Her mouth drops. "That's it? No reason for why he did it? You deserve at least that."

"He tried. I wouldn't let him. I didn't feel strong enough to sit through all the details. It hurt too much."

With wide eyes, she massages her temples. "There's so much to take in. I'm just ... really shocked."

"I probably shouldn't have said anything, but it feels good to have someone to talk to. It's been hard holding it all in."

"Are you kidding? I'm glad you told me." She pulls me into hug. "I'm a little pissed you waited so long."

"I know ... It's just that I—"

"I forgive you," she interrupts, placing her hands on my shoulders. "And I feel like you and Luke still need to talk ... get some answers. If anything, it'll bring you closure." We turned our heads at the sound of the door, finding Logan with a goofy grin on his face, looking back and forth between us.

"Am I interrupting something?" he asks, making his way over.

"You're fine," I sniff, before forcing a smile. I'd said what needed to be said.

"You sure?" Gia asks hesitantly.

I tip my head toward Logan. "Go give your man some love already. I'm about ready for bed."

His arms stretch wide, and she meets him with a kiss. He makes sure to use lots of tongue, then finally lets her go. "You ladies ready for Vegas?"

Gia and I both smile.

"Hell yeah!" He wiggles his brows. "'Cause I just booked our suite."

We squeal excitedly. Our trip to Sin City has been planned for nearly a month, and it couldn't have come at a better time. We're going to a highly anticipated UFC fight, spend a couple days lounging around the pool, and I'm sure we'll do some shopping.

"Two more weeks! It'll be here before we know it," Gia says before her face falls. "I wish you were heading down there with us. I need you on that plane."

"I'll be there, holding your hand, baby. Nothing's going to happen," Logan soothes.

"Thanks, but it's not the same. I need you both. No offense," she replies.

He rolls his eyes.

If there's anything Gia's afraid of, it's flying. I'm surprised she agreed to get on a plane in the first place. I guess that's what you do when you're in love—step out of your comfort zone to make the other person happy.

"Enjoy your time alone while you have it. Sean and I will be there the next day."

Logan looks pleased by this. "I made sure the rooms are conjoined. You okay sharing a bed with him? There's always the couch."

"That's fine. And thanks for asking." *If I don't want to have sex with him, I won't. I don't think the number of beds will make a difference*. The clock reads 7:40, but it feels three hours later. I yawn. "I'm going to bed, guys. I'm tired."

"It's early," Logan replies.

"Think it's the wine," I yell over my shoulder as I head toward my room. "Enjoy the rest of your night. See you guys in the morning."

"Goodnight," Gia replies, then I dive onto my bed, falling into a peaceful slumber.

Chapter
REESE
Five

"Hey sleepyhead," Sean says, sitting next to me. I didn't expect to see him. He'd told me he'd been up to his ears in work and wouldn't be able to make it tonight.

I throw off my comforter, a lazy smile creeping over my face. "I thought you had to work. What time is it?" The clock reads just past eleven.

He's wearing a dark gray shirt with low-slung jeans, and I breathe in his citrusy scent. He presses a chaste kiss to my lips. "I do, but I had to see you."

"Oh?" I ask, stretching. "You missed me that much, huh?"

"Yeah, I did."

"Logan booked our suites today."

"I heard. You excited?" His fingers gently stroke my arm.

"Of course! How could I not be? Are they still up?"

"They're watching a movie." He kisses me again, slowly this time, but I pull back. His eyes look a little sad.

"Are you excited?" We haven't talked about the trip since we first made the plans.

"Yeah." His reply lacks any enthusiasm.

"Doesn't sound like it." I frown, scooting over to give him some room, and he lies

down beside me, kicking off his shoes.

"Sorry," he sighs. "Just got a lot on my mind."

"Did you get enough work done?"

He shrugs. "I made a small dent, then decided you were more important. How

'bout you?" he asks, rubbing small circles over my back, his expression cautious. "How'd work go today?"

I can't help but feel a little bad. I don't want to make a big deal out of it.

"All right, I guess. Nothing too exciting."

"Really?" he asks, laughing softly. "I was expecting at least a story or two."

"Sorry to disappoint." I nuzzle him.

Dipping his head in for a kiss, he slips his tongue deep into my mouth, groaning. "I know a way you can make me feel better."

"Oh yeah?" I wrap my hand around his neck, kissing him back.

"Want me to show you?" His fingers tease my skin where the hem of my shirt meets my thighs. My heart rate increases, but I try to relax.

"Why yes. I think I do."

"Good. I was hoping you'd say that," he replies, using one arm to take off his shirt, before doing the same to mine. Then he's cupping my breasts, flicking his thumbs back and forth over my nipples, watching them harden. "See?" He grins. "Already starting to feel better."

"Glad I can be of service," I breathe.

His jeans fall to the floor, then his palm presses over the center of my panties. We've gone from zero to sixty in seconds.

"Is this the reason you came over?" I ask on a shaky breath.

He removes my panties, pushing two fingers inside me, and I tense.

"I'm not going to say it wasn't a motivator," he groans, stroking my sensitive flesh. "Damn, you're tight."

I clench my teeth because it hurts, and he slows down his movements.

"You okay?" he asks, eyes pleading for me to let him continue.

"I ... I think so." When I'd done this with Luke, I'd been ready. This time feels entirely different.

Sean senses my distraction. "Stay with me, Reese." His voice is gentle. "I know you want this." He pushes his fingers in and out of me at a steady pace.

I try to do what he says. *"We're adults. We love each other."*

He gazes down on me with hungry eyes. "Do you like this?"

"It feels good," I tell him, trying to focus. It *does* feel good, now that my body's getting used to him, but I still feel something is missing—some sort of connection. *Would sex be the answer? Is that all it is? And if it were, why had it felt right with Luke? It'd always felt right with Luke. Who am I kidding? I shouldn't trust my own instincts.*

"Did he bother you? Touch you in a way to make you uncomfortable?"

Huh? "Who?" That's an odd question to be asking, considering what we're doing.

"You know who I'm talking about."

I blink. *Did he know what I was thinking?* "Is it really the time to ask?" I gently push him off me. "Way to kill the mood, Sean."

He rolls over. "Don't pretend like you were into it."

"I *had* been ... until you opened your mouth. Great timing by the way." *Truthfully, I'm relieved.*

His brows bunch together. "What happened to you? You're a vibrant, twenty-one year old woman. You're sexy as hell, yet you have little-to-no sexual experience."

"Are you complaining?"

"No." He blows out a breath. "I'm not trying to pressure you. I'm trying to communicate." Holding up his hands, he asks, "Do you even want to be with me? Be honest."

"Yes!" I say convincingly.

"'Cause a moment ago, you were some place else." He rests his head in his hands. "Tell me, Reese. Where'd you go?"

"I—I don't know." If I tell him the truth, it'll crush him. I drop my gaze to his chest, which is still glistening with sweat. "It happens sometimes. My mind just sort of drifts." I hate liars, and now I've become one. I know exactly where I was. *With the tattooed, six foot three Adonis who resides across the way.* I tell myself there are times we have no control over our thoughts, in an attempt to lesson the guilt I'm feeling, but it doesn't seem to help.

"And you avoided my question," he says quietly. "Did he touch you?"

My eyes flick back to his. "What do you mean, did he touch me? He isn't some sort of pervert, Sean." *He doesn't know Luke the way I do – nothing about our history or how he had saved me years ago.*

"I told you I don't trust him with you."

"I know you don't."

"Why are you defending him then?"

My gaze softens. "Because he was a gentleman, Sean. You have no reason to worry. My heart belongs to you now," I say sincerely, planting a gentle kiss on his lips. "Can we talk about something else?" My phone chimes with a message, but I ignore it. Whoever it is can wait.

"Go ahead," he says, eyeing it.

"No way. We're talking."

"What if it's important?"

I shrug. "They can wait."

Looking at me skeptically, he reaches for it, but I grab it and toss it onto my nightstand. "What is your problem?"

"Why won't you check it?"

I frown, narrowing my eyes. "I told you, we are talking."

"You just don't want me to see it. That's what it is!" This is getting ridiculous.

"I want you to trust me. I thought it'd be rude to check in the middle of our conversation. But you want me to check. Fine, I'll check!" Grabbing my phone, I hand it over. "Better yet, *you* check." I have nothing to hide now that the flowers are out in the open.

Gladly jerking it out of my hand, his eyes roam over the text. His face turns three shades of violet. He says nothing when he gives it back.

My gaze falls on the text, then I swallow before I can look at him again. "It's the first time he's messaged me since he's been back. I swear."

He gets out of bed quickly and puts on his clothes. "I need to go. You should text him back. Don't want to keep him waiting."

"Sean—"

He won't even look at me. "I'll see you later, Reese."

"You *do* believe me, don't you?"

He doesn't reply, and this time I decide to let him go.

Chapter

REESE

Six

Thump, thump, thump is the only sound I hear when I step inside the gym. Luke stands in the back, rhythmically pounding his fists into the heavy bag, left-right, left-right, left-right.

"I didn't think you'd show," he says, his expression never wavering. I'm surprised he even knew I was here.

It took ten minutes of cursing and beating on my steering wheel to get my stalled Civic out on the street. Thank God it finally started, and I wasn't sitting in traffic. "I had car troubles."

"That's not what I meant." He continues to swing with brutal force. Beads of sweat drip from his temple. I watch his chest rise and fall, hoping he brought an extra shirt. The one he's wearing is soaked and clinging to him, which could be a bit of a distraction. When he's finished with the bag I finally have his full attention. His eyes travel from the top of my head to the tips of my toes. He doesn't bother being discreet about it.

My skin warms, and I try to look unaffected. I'm wearing gray yoga pants, a soft pink tank, and my hair is thrown into a messy bun. I didn't fuss with putting on make-up. It's far too early for that, but he's making me feel self-conscious. "What?" *Not all of us look like a god in the wee hours of the morning.*

He discards his gloves, then we both tread toward the cage. "Your car's a piece of shit," he says, a little short of breath. "You need a new one." He wipes the sweat from his brow.

"It's easier said than done for some people." I give him a sideways glance.

"I'll get my buddy to look at it. See if he can fix it." He acts like this is a no-brainer.

"You don't have to help me." *You're not my boyfriend. Remember?*

"I'll get him to look at it," he replies like I don't have a choice. "The idea of you alone, stuck in a broken down car doesn't sit well with me. Sorry."

To tell you the truth, it doesn't sit well with me either. I decide not to argue.

Pulling his shirt over his head, he uses it to wipe the sweat off his body.

I spot a scar on his shoulder—one I've never seen and want to ask about—but he distracts me when he works his way down his stomach. His carved V flexes and disappears below his waistband.

I need a glass of water. *Forgive me Father, for I have sinned. Keep it together, Reese! Eyes on the face!*

"Did you tell him?"

Confused, my forehead creases.

"Your boy," he clarifies. "Does he know where you are? Who you're with?"

"I'm not discussing Sean with you."

"He doesn't like us working together. Does he?" A wry grin spreads on his face. His smugness agitates me.

I lift my chin. "You're one to talk."

"How's that?"

"Privately training with an ex. *That* isn't going to be a problem?"

"For? Unless you're referring to Chance, I've got no one to answer to." Tossing his shirt out of the way, he continues, "That's the luxury of being single," he adds flatly.

I blink until it registers, then my words are jumbled. "I ... I'm sorry. I didn't..."

"Don't apologize."

Closing my mouth, I focus on the floor. An awkward silence falls between us. *That explains her absence.* Retying my shoes so I don't have to look at him, I wonder if he notices my shaky hands. *Did he love her? Did he ever truly love me? This is all just so confusing.*

"Why'd you come?" he asks, bringing me out of my thoughts.

Why'd I come? Why did *I come? Good question.* Keeping my emotions in check, I say, "I've gotten rusty since you've been gone. Stopped training, stopped caring." I exhale a long breath. "I'm doing it for the kids." *Not for you, if that's what you're asking.*

He watches me intently, and it penetrates my bones, awakening something within me. He can do that with just a look. It's an unfair advantage, and I feel naked.

"What?"

"Nothing," he replies, shaking his head as if to clear it. "You want to start where we left off?"

My gaze narrows on his tan, muscled chest. "Seriously?"

A brow arches in question. "Yeah. There a problem?"

"You're not wearing a shirt."

He grabs the sweaty shirt off the floor and puts an arm through.

"You don't have another?"

Pulling it over his head, it's still obviously wet. "I didn't think you'd show."

"Leave it off then. I guess."

"I'll wear it, if you want."

"Keep it off."

Tossing it behind him, he strides toward me, looking as if he's battling something. Then he takes my chin in his hand. I think I stopped breathing before he even touched me. His thumb glides across my bottom lip, and his eyes follow the movement. "You're nervous," he says, just above a whisper.

Unable to speak, I nod in admission. Even after all that sweating, I can smell a hint of his body wash mixed with his manly scent. *He's no good for you. You've moved on.*

"Why?" he asks.

"I—I don't know." *Why'd you choose her? Was it worth it? Do you have any*

regrets?

The corner of his mouth tips. "Don't worry. I'll be gentle."

I force a smile, pretending that'll solve everything.

☆ ☆ ☆

We've gone through several types of chokeholds. In this one, we're standing with my back pressed against the cage. Luke's hands are wrapped around me, lightly squeezing. I raise my right hand high and turn my body to the left, bringing my arm down quickly. This traps Luke's arms under mine, but is meant to loosen his grip a little. With my free arm, I swing my elbow toward his face. I didn't expect to make contact, but there's a crack, and Luke grunts, stumbling over.

My eyes widen, and I look for blood. "Are you okay?" Unable to find any, I breathe a sigh of relief. He can't be hurt that bad, though I really felt it.

He backs away with a light chuckle, covering his face. "I'm fine."

"Let me see it. Does it hurt?" I try to move his arm, but he won't let me.

"If I say yes, are you going to take care of me?"

When I frown, he chuckles again.

"Nah, if anything, you shocked me." He moves his hand, and his right eye shows faint bruising already. I got him good.

A new wave of confidence rolls over me. "Maybe next time you'll pay better attention. Looks like you'll have a shiner."

His eyes drift to mine. "Yeah, well maybe you distract me."

My cheeks heat, but I pretend I didn't hear him, offering to get him an ice pack.

He kindly declines, then cracks his neck from side to side. "Don't act like you don't enjoy this," he says, breaking the tension. I fight a smirk, but he sees it. "Uh huh."

"Okay, I'll admit it feels good, but just a little."

Crossing his arms with an unreadable expression, his feet are shoulder width apart. "You ready to keep going?"

My brows lift to my forehead. "Can you handle it? Now that you're injured, I mean?"

He barks out a laugh. "I'll show you what I can handle."

"Let's go then." I grin.

☆☆☆

A half-hour in and I'm sweating. Luke's got me pinned flat on my back, his chest pressing against mine. I don't think his ego's going to let me win this time.

"You sure you don't want to start over?" His tone is light as I try to move him off me.

"Why would I want that?" I gasp, my energy near depleted.

His laughter blows against my skin, and my body reacts, spreading goose bumps all over my flesh. My body's a traitor. I'm angry—angry for liking this too much, angry that I can't concentrate with his shirtless body between my legs, angry that every second I lie here, I have to remind myself of what he did, of how he betrayed me, of how I won't do the same to Sean. And finally, I'm angry that he smells so devastatingly delicious.

"You're wasting a lot of energy getting angry."

"Pssh, I'm not angry." I squirm, panting, wishing he couldn't hear how tired I am.

"Then you're frustrated."

"Only because you're talking," I say, hooking my foot underneath him. His face is way too close. I want to flip him over, but know that I don't have a chance. I'm too exhausted.

"Do you want me to stop?"

"Talking?" I lift my hips, doing a crunch, trying to get enough space between us. So I can push him off. It doesn't work. "Yes! Please, stop." I'm too stubborn to give up.

"Focus on your breathing. You're too tense."

I lift my hips and grunt. "Can't you see that I'm trying?" I'm disgusted that I sound like a baby, but I'm panicking. I can't catch my breath, and I feel helpless. Flickers of my past start to haunt me. I'm losing all control.

"Look at me," he says sternly, and I do, staring at him like he's my lifeline.

"Relax," he says more softly. "Breathe with me." I feel his steady heartbeat beating through his chest. Together we breathe in sync, in through the nose, out through the mouth.

"You're doing good," he whispers." Keep breathing."

"I got you," he says, untying my trembling hands. He rubs gentle circles over my wrists, then glances at my face before turning to give me

some privacy. I pull up my shorts and panties, letting him know when I am decent. He scans all my tiny cuts from the glass. "Can you walk?"

When I nod, he orders that I wait across the street.

Shaking my head, I don't budge. I won't budge, not without him.

"He won't touch you. You're safe. It's just until the cops arrive."

"I don't want to be alone." My voice is unrecognizable.

His gaze fixes on Ronald. He's bound, gagged, and blindfolded on the floor. Luke had threatened to blow him to pieces. "You shouldn't be anywhere near this shit stain," he says with his jaw clenched tight. I think he's going to make me leave.

Tears roll down the sides of my cheeks. "I don't want to be alone," I say again,

choking back a sob.

"Shh. It's okay." He sits, stretching out his legs. "We'll wait together. I won't let

him hurt you," he soothes beside me, wrapping an arm around my shoulders, making me feel safe. "I'm here." He presses his lips to the top of my head. "I'm just sorry I didn't get here sooner."

"You okay?" Luke brushes a tear from my cheek. The gentle gesture only confuses me, and I roll my eyes to keep the rest from falling, "No," I sniff. He's still lying between my legs. With a heavy heart I just stare at him, trying to figure out why. "No. I'm not okay, Luke." How could he do this to me? I've trusted him since I was eight years old. "You've ruined me. You know that?"

His face falls, and he moves off me, placing his head in his hands. His hair's sticking up through his fingers.

I keep my tongue at the roof of my mouth, trying not to break down in front of him. "You've taken a piece of my heart that I'll never get back. How could you do this to me?" It's hard to get the words out. "I keep going over the past. It's all just so confusing," I say, biting my lower lip. "You can't possibly understand how much you've hurt me. Blindsided me the way that you did. I ... I thought you loved me."

His head snaps up. "I *do* love you." He swallows. "God, I love you more than anything." The anguish on his face makes my heart constrict.

"I don't know if I can do this. I need time to think."

Looking pained, he says, "I'm sorry. I'll say it every day for the rest of my life, and I know that still won't be enough."

I move toward the exit, and then as fast as I can to my car. "Stupid! Stupid! Stupid!" I hiss. Once it's unlocked, I climb in and slam the door shut. When cranking the engine, I hear a click then nothing else. *C'mon, c'mon. Don't do this to me.* Cranking it again, I yell, "Shit!" I slap my palm against the steering wheel, accidentally blowing the horn. The driver door opens, and I don't need to look to know who it is. I can feel him whenever he's near me. Not to mention it's still too early for anyone else to be around.

"Sounds like the battery. Need a ride?"

I glance at him out of the corner of my eye, then slowly nod. Could this be any more humiliating?

He watches me from under his lashes. "We're gonna have to take my bike."

Resting my hands in my lap, I fight more tears. "That's fine." I used to not be a crier, but I swear he brings it out of me. I've never cried more tears than I do for this man.

When he holds out a hand, I take it, climbing out of my car, before I move past him.

He walks behind me. "Let's go home."

Chapter
LUKE
Seven

I haven't talked to her since that morning her car broke down, when I'd given her a ride on my Harley. It had gutted me, seeing how much I'd hurt her. I'd been surprised she'd agreed to let me take her home.

She hesitates before climbing on the back of my bike. I place a helmet over her head, tightening her chinstrap. She works hard at holding back her tears, chewing on her lip the way that she does.

"Stop hiding them," I tell her. "I deserve to see them. For Christ's sake ... I put 'em there." *After all these years, you'd think we'd be past this.*

She nervously wraps her arms around me, interlocking her delicate fingers. "It's embarrassing, being emotional in front of someone else. When I was a kid, I was taught that crying was a sign of weakness." *She scoots up so that her thighs press snuggly against my hips. I close my eyes, savoring the feeling.*

"Who told you that?"

"My father."

I'm not even sure why I asked. I already knew the answer. Maybe

I just wanted to hear her voice. "He was a drunk back then. He didn't mean it." Glancing over my shoulder at her beautiful face, I add, "If he were still alive he'd tell you that. You meant the world to him, Reese."

"You're right. He would." She inhales a deep breath, then slowly blows it out. "But I've cried enough tears over you."

I get it. You've made it clear. "I don't want you to feel like you can't talk to me."

"I can't talk to you." She averts her eyes. "Please, can we just go?"

I rev the engine, honoring her wishes. Neither of us speak the whole way home.

The next day I replace the battery in her piece of shit car. If I said her shock didn't sting a bit, I'd been lying. What does it take for the woman to realize what she means to me — the lengths I would go to make her happy? I'm convinced the boyfriend had something to do with her nixing the private lessons. He doesn't like our working together, worried I'm gonna take back what he took from me. All I know is I don't trust him, and I'm not alone in that opinion. Logan's had his number from the get-go.

"What about you, boy?" I ask my furry best friend, rubbing the top of his head. "You don't like him either, huh?" He whimpers and his ears perk up, but then he's back to chewing on his toy. The front door swings open, and Logan strides in with a couple of beers, looking like he needs to talk. I lift my chin, and he hands one over after twisting off the cap.

"Dude, you're gonna need this."

I gesture to the lazy boy across from me. "Take a seat."

"Can't stay long. Gia and I are headed up to Heartland's for happy hour. Come up." He bends over and pats Chance on the head. "Hey buddy, what you got there?" He glances my way before adding, "Sean and Reese are goin'."

"Thanks, man. I'll pass."

"You might change your mind after you hear this."

"I can't be around that prick."

"Dude, listen." His eyes go wide. "You know how I told you about Gia being a pain in the ass lately—accusing me of shit for no reason."

I nod, taking a pull from the bottle. It's all he ever talks about.

"Two weeks to the date ... there's been no sex, bro. She thinks I'm keeping secrets. One day we were talking about the future, marriage, poppin' out a couple of kids. The next, she's going on about bros before hos. Not making any sense."

I try to process all that, still going over the marriage part and Logan. "Must have done something to piss her off." I take another swig. "Talk to her, find out what's setting her off." Not like *I'm* the expert. *That's a joke.*

"I'm getting to that. Hold up. It's sort of a long story," he says, finally sitting down. "So today we're at the house. I'm trying to get laid, and she's pushing me away again. I get pissed. She never used to refuse me. My mind starts going, and I'm wondering if she's fuckin' someone else, so I ask her." I choke out a laugh. *I'm sure that went over well.* "Yeah, I know ... she was so pissed, she slapped me. Anyway, she finally tells me why I'm on her shit list. And bro, here's the crazy part. Before I start, you don't have anything to tell me?" he asks, cocking one of his brows at me.

I pause with the beer against my lips. "I'm not following. What does this have to do with me?"

"*Dude...*" He snickers. "Your girl seems to think you were married."

My forehead wrinkles, and I wait for the punch line.

"I'm *dead* serious. And what's worse is she told Gia you admitted it. That's why I had to ask."

"The fuck you talkin' about? Admitted what?" I rest my elbows on my knees. "Grab me a beer, will ya?" I look around for the cameras, wondering if I'm being *Punk'd* or something, cause this shit is crazy.

"That's pretty much how I responded, man," he said, handing me my drink. "She said Reese has met the girl—once at the hospital and once coming out of your house. Introduced herself as Rachelle or some shit like that. Thinks you two were fooling around when you left."

My eyes swing to his. "You've got to be shittin' me. Rachelle did this?"

"So this woman exists?"

"Fuck yeah, she exists. She's an agent, who's got a thing for me, but I've never touched the woman!" I groan, irritated, remembering the nurse calling her my wife when I was in the hospital. It pisses me off that Reese would think I'd actually do that to her. Shaking my head, I ask, "She's sayin' I admitted this?"

He nods. "Said you apologized the night you came back."

"Well damn." I rest my head back against the couch, remembering the words she and I exchanged that night. I *had* apologized, but it'd been about her father. *Wait.* "Does she ever talk about Andrew around you? What she knows about his death?"

He shrugs. "No, not really. I stay clear of the subject like you'd asked."

"Gia ever say anything about it?"

"Just that the Feds wouldn't release any names. Told Reese it was for safety reasons. She knows his killer is dead."

He's dead all right. And I'd kill him again with no regrets.

Relief and apprehension pour over me. If what he's saying is true, all the hatred I've gotten from Reese has been about Rachelle.

Damn! I could fucking strangle the woman. My grip tightens on the bottle. "You said Reese met her twice ... my imaginary wife?"

He laughs. "That's what Gia told me."

I can only imagine all that Rachelle said to her; that woman is a schemer. "What time you guys heading up?"

His eyes light up, and he checks his phone. "In about an hour. You gonna go?"

"Thinkin' about it." I rub my chin.

"Dude, you should."

"Do me a favor. Don't say anything to Gia. Send her over before you go, and I'll clear the air with her."

Chapter LUKE Eight

Back in Gia's good graces, I shower and clean up before heading down to the brewery. She'd bombarded me with her questions, and I figured it'd be best if I didn't beat around the bush. My answers had shocked the hell out of her. She'd cried over the fact that I'd shot my dad, calling me a hero. I'd told her I didn't deserve the title. The real hero is the man I couldn't save — the father of the woman I love. It'll be on my conscience the rest of my life.

Gia did what she could, to get me to see Reese's side of the misunderstanding. Doesn't mean I'm not hurt or angry over the lack of trust she has in me. She'd run off with the neighbor, giving him time that should've been mine — letting him touch her, kiss her, and whatever else he's done with her. Yeah, I'd say I'm pretty pissed, and I plan to play with her head a bit before I give her the truth.

Now we're sitting in the back of the bar, and the person I came to see isn't here yet. The douchebag mentioned her mother had called unexpectedly, so she'd be running a few minutes late.

That was nearly an hour ago. My eyes keep roaming over to the entrance, expecting to see her walk in.

Her boyfriend wasn't happy when I'd taken the seat across from him. I reveled in the clear disappointment on his face. He'd been shocked to see me, and I've watched him pound back four or five beers since then. He hasn't put any effort into joining our conversation either, which is fine by me. I'd rather he sit quiet the rest of the night. It'll help me keep my fists to myself.

Logan sits beside me, and Gia next to him—obviously on better terms than earlier; in fact, they're so close they've got their chairs touching.

"Book your room yet, brotha?" Logan asks, hounding me about Vegas. I'm not thrilled about the idea of hangin' with the four of them, but now that I know what I know, I'm starting to consider it.

I cross my arms over my chest, letting out a breath. "Still haven't decided."

He looks disappointed. "Decide, man. Time's runnin' out."

"I've got a couple days."

"You *have* to. It'll be fun!" Gia joins in. "We'll lay by the pool, drink dirty martinis," I roll my eyes, and she adds, "Drink whatever you want. It's going to be a good time."

Maybe it will. Maybe it won't.

"Everything's got to be booked already," comes from Sean across the table.

We all stare at him. Funny he chose this time to offer his opinion.

His eyes move between us. "What?"

"You afraid of a little competition?" I lean back in my chair.

"Just trying to save you time. The fight isn't the only event in Vegas next week. It's going to be packed."

"Don't matter," Logan retorts. "We got a couch in our suite. Worst-case scenario, you sleep on that." He flashes his teeth. Sean guzzles the rest of his beer, avoiding eye contact, hating the idea of my going.

I slip my straw into my mouth, watching him closely. "I'll think about it."

"Accept it, man. You're going." Logan grabs his empty mug and looks around the bar. "I need another beer. Where the fuck's our waitress?"

"Be nice," Gia scolds.

The waitress appears a moment later. "Sorry it took me so long. Your server must have left in a hurry, and she transferred your table without letting me know. You guys ready for another round?" She uses a pitcher to fill up our waters.

"*Yes,*" Logan replies dramatically, drumming his knuckles on the table. "I'll take another Sierra Nevada. Make sure it's a tall."

She digs out a pad of paper and writes it down, before her eyes move to Gia. "For you?"

"Ignore my boyfriend. He's slow," she says, making me chuckle. "I'll have another Dirty Martini, please."

"Thanks for the warning," she smiles sweetly. "Oh … hey you!"

I blink, recognizing her long blonde hair and heart-shaped face. Scooting out of my chair, I greet her with an awkward side-hug. "Brandi, what are you doing here?" Last I'd heard she was living in Flagstaff with my sister. They're attending college together … at least they were at one point.

"It's sort of a long story." Her blue eyes move about the bar. "I'll fill you in when it dies down a little. My tables are all filling up, and I'm running behind."

"No problem. Do what you got to do."

She smirks. "You'll have to go easy on me. I'm still learning."

I swing my thumb over to Logan. "The only one you need to worry about is this guy over here."

He whacks me with a menu. "You know he's full of shit, right?"

"I'm sure I'll find out soon enough," she replies, her eyes shining. Pointing at my mug, she asks, "What about you? Want another beer?"

"Not yet, but there's one more joining us. Can you bring her a water?"

"Sure!" Flicking her gaze over to Sean, she adds, "Last but not least, can I interest you in a drink?"

By the lust in his eyes, you'd think she was standing buck-naked.

"*Sir*, would you like another drink?" Her cheeks turn pink while she waits for him.

"Yes, I would," he finally says, focusing on her tits.

She smiles coyly. "*Okaayy*, can you tell me what it is, so I can bring it out for you?"

"I'll take another Black & Tan," he winks, tipping his mug. Someone needs to cut this prick off.

What the hell was that? I toss a glance at Gia and Logan, but they're too into each other to notice, scooting out of their chairs. Logan rests a hand on the small of her back, pushing her forward.

"She left her phone in the car," he smirks, leaning in. "It'll be quick, man. I need this."

You've got to be kidding me. I narrow my eyes at him. "You know that ain't smart." *Leaving us here like this.*

"Look, I'm 'bout ready to shoot in my pants. You gonna help me out with it?"

"Fuck no."

"Well, there you go. All I need is two minutes."

"Better hurry your pecker along then." I glance at Gia, who now has her hands on

her hips, probably wondering why we're arguing. She doesn't even know what she's in for. "I'm startin' the clock," I tell him.

He turns away and rushes her toward the exit. I readjust my hat and focus on one of the many televisions, unable to look at this guy without contemplating violence.

A woman comes stumbling toward our table, wearing a condom hanging from her necklace and a crown on top of her head that displays the words, *Bride To Be*.

"Sorry to bother you," she says shyly. "My friends dared me to ask."

I glance toward her friends, who are watching from several feet behind her … all of them are giggling. I'm almost afraid to hear the question.

A grin tugs at her lips. "Are you Luke Ryann?"

I'm surprised she can see what's in front of her. "Yes I am," I tell her, amused.

"I knew it! Would you mind if I gave you a hug? My fiancé's a huge fan." She sways to the right, gripping the table for balance. "I promise to leave you alone after that." She looks back at her friends, and a few of them wave.

I ponder the possibility that I may be wearing her vomit, but don't want to come across as a dick. So I give the 'Bride To Be' what she wants, congratulate her on her nuptials, and allow her friends to snap some pictures.

Sean tips his head toward the same women, after they've left us alone. "Bet my left nut you could score a blow job from the bachelorette."

"Not interested."

"In blow jobs?"

"In the bachelorette." *Stupid prick.* "But I think you already know that." Logan better hurry his ass up.

Brandi comes back and hands Sean his beer, though it's clear he doesn't need it. She sets the rest of our drinks on the table. "Did I scare everyone away?"

I shake my head. "Nah, they're coming back."

She looks confused, eyes moving between us. "Then why the long faces."

"The guest of honor isn't here yet." My gaze flicks to Sean's, and we have some sort of stare off.

Brandi shuffles her feet. "*I see.*" She glances behind her toward a table of rowdy customers. "Well I'm… gonna go check on my other tables. Give me a holler if you need anything," then she scurries away.

Sean's eyes follow the back of her, which isn't a surprise. "How do you know her?"

It takes a moment to answer. "Why do you care?" *What does Reese see in you anyway?*

"Just making conversation."

"I saw the way you looked at her."

Bringing his mug to his lips, he pauses. "Last time I checked, there was nothing wrong with looking, my *friend*." He takes a sip. "Don't pretend like you haven't." A wry smirk spreads over his face. I imagine rearranging it. He's lucky we're in public.

I lean into the table, locking my fingers, "I'm going to speak *very* clearly, so you understand. *You and I aren't friends.*"

"Well, I appreciate you clearing that up."

"I'll clear up something else. If you do anything to hurt Reese—if there's one single hair on her head out of place, I'll knock out all your teeth and wear them as a necklace."

He spits out a bitter laugh. "Let me remind you: she came to me. She doesn't want you anymore. You're making yourself look pathetic."

"Call it whatever you want, but I'm taking back what you stole from me."

Logan strides over. "Look who decided to show up!"

Chapter
REESE
Nine

After five attempts to reach Sean, I give up and shoot him a quick text: *GRRR... BE THERE IN TEN.*

I'd pulled over in the grocery store parking lot, afraid of breaking down again. It's not the battery. The noise is different—more like a grinding instead of a click. The thing is falling apart on me.

Gia and I had planned to get the men together before our trip, in hopes that they'd bond so things aren't awkward between them. My mother had called before I stepped into the shower, which is why I'm running behind.

"Heartland's Brewery," I tell the driver, having no choice but to call a cab. The place is right down the street, but I didn't plan on walking in these stilettos. I'm already feeling out of my element, having originally planned to wear jeans, until Gia intervened, laying one of her outfits out on my bed.

"*Wear this. You'll look gorgeous!*" *she says, beaming.*

I am too busy noticing how stunning she looks in her lipstick red dress. Her hair is pulled back in an elegant fashion, showing off her high cheekbones and glowing features.

My eyes drop to my jeans. "Wow, you look — "

"Thank you. It's new ... and I don't plan on changing," she replies seriously. "Don't even think about wearing those jeans. You're dressing up tonight." Her heels click on my bathroom floor, then she disappears into my closet.

I glance down on my bed, finding a plum bohemian top that falls off the shoulder, and a short, black fitted skirt. "Gia, you're crazy! I can't fit into your clothes!"

She prances through the bathroom, dangling my black strappy stilettos from her fingers, then sets them down in front of me. "These will go perfect! Wear your hair down, and make it wavy. I told Logan I want to leave early to beat the crowd."

"I still need to shower."

"We'll drive separate. I don't want to be stuck without a table. See you up there." She waves, closing my door.

☆☆☆

I inhale a long, slow breath, wondering how the rest of the night will play out. Sean's insecurity has been putting a wrench in our relationship. He's distant, drowning himself in work. The only way I can explain it is that neither of us are happy. I'm just hanging on to the chance that things will get better between us, and he'll eventually get off my case about Luke.

And therein lies the problem.

Luke.

I'm not ready to let him go, and, truthfully, I don't know if I'll ever be — not completely. There's too much history between us. I'm realizing that. Regardless of his hurtful choices, the good outweighs the bad, and he's been a part of my life for too many years to just write him off. I don't think I'm capable.

"You hear they're lookin' for a murder suspect?"

I glance at the elderly man in the rearview, his expression concerned, as he drops the volume on the radio down to a low hum.

"Around here?"

"Yep." He nods. "Grocery store parking lot, back where I picked you up. Cameras caught the attack. Suspect snatched the girl yesterday."

"They already know she was murdered?" Chills creep up the back of my neck, and I shiver, rubbing my arms. I can't help but think of the pick-up truck, with the foil over the windows. I'm sure I'm just being paranoid, but the thought still comes to my mind. The first time I'd seen it was in that very parking lot. It'd been parked right next to my car.

"Yes, ma'am. Found a body in the desert, a few miles from where he took her. So be on the lookout for anything suspicious," he warns. "The suspect had his face covered, and they don't have many leads."

"What about the getaway vehicle?"

"They're not even sure there was one. Turns out a camera was broken."

I shake my head, covering my mouth. I know these things happen, but this is just too close to home. "How old was she? Did they say?"

"Judging by the pictures, I'd have to guess around your age — maybe a little younger. Late teens probably."

"I hope they find him."

"You and me both. They haven't identified the body, but they're assuming..." He trails off, gripping the steering wheel so tightly that his knuckles turn white.

"Assuming it's most likely her," I say, finishing his sentence, thinking of the horror she must have endured during her final hours. I send up a silent prayer for her. "Thank you for telling me. As you can see, I'm a little behind on current events."

"That'll change when you're old and wrinkled like me."

We pull in front of the restaurant, where a number of people stand in front of the double doors—probably waiting for their tables. I guess Gia was right. "Hope I didn't ruin your night."

"Are you kidding me? Not at all. You may have saved my life." I pay the fee and add a generous tip. "I'll be sure to lock all my windows and doors."

"Atta girl!" he grins. "Now you be careful, miss."

"Will do!" I wave, then make my way toward the entrance, stepping inside the crowded restaurant.

The dimly lit bar is off to the right. I don't see anyone in my party yet, but that's expected. The restaurant is huge, and people are everywhere. When I stride toward the back, what looks like a bachelorette party is standing around the bar, blocking my view of more tables. "Excuse me," I tell them politely.

"Where have you been, woman? We've been here over an hour!" a male voice yells from behind me. I glance over my shoulder, finding Logan and Gia hand in hand, their faces flushed. "Glad you made it. We were just getting ready to leave."

"Leave her alone," Gia scolds. "He's teasing. Is everything okay? You look stressed."

"I'll let you know, once I have my wine. Why aren't you two at a table? Where's Sean?"

"Simmer down, woman. We'll take you to him," Logan answers, pulling Gia behind him, squeezing through the group of women, toward the high-top tables in the back. I expect to find Sean alone, but it's the person seated across from him who captures my attention. He's got his hat pulled down real low, and he's glaring at Sean like he wants to rip him apart.

Oh my God. Sean is going to kill me.

I pinch the back of Logan's shirt, jerking him back. "What the hell is *he* doing here?" I hiss, nearly stumbling over.

He straightens his shoulders. "You got a problem? I invited him last minute," he says, clearly offended I dared to ask.

"A little warning would've been nice!"

He can invite whomever he wants, but I would've liked to have been prepared for this.

I glance over at Gia, who's conveniently avoiding my eyes. We'll definitely be

having a talk after this. *Why hadn't she told me?*

"Look who decided to show up." Logan gives Luke a high-five then sits down beside him.

When Luke peers up at me, my insides come alive in a way that should *not* be happening. I acknowledge him with a polite nod then take the seat next to Sean, as if this setting is normal for us.

Chapter

REESE

Ten

"Sorry I'm late," I manage to say evenly. "Anyone else starving?" I grab a menu with shaky hands and hide behind it, giving Sean a quick peck. It feels wrong for Luke to have to see it.

"I am now," Logan grumbles.

Sean rests his hand on my thigh. "Fifteen minutes my ass. What took you so long?" His breath smells of stale beer, and it looks like he's already had a lot to drink.

"If you'd have answered your phone earlier, you wouldn't have to ask," I snap back. Glancing at him sideways, I add, "I'll fill you in soon enough. Let me order my wine first."

He pulls his phone out of his pocket and squints, struggling to read my messages. "Shit! My ringer was off. Are you pissed?"

"No. I'm hungry. And are you seriously drunk already?" I guess I can't blame him, though, given the situation he's in.

"We've been here an hour. What did you expect?"

"Had her bring you a water," Luke points, stealing my attention.

I find it odd that *he's* the one who ordered it, but I thank him and take a sip. A half grin appears on his face. I look away 'cause it makes me warm and tingly.

"Where the fuck's your friend, Luke? We're hungry." Logan scans the restaurant. I wasn't aware that Luke invited someone.

"Would you use some manners for once?" Gia glares.

"What?"

"Get your panties out of a wad. She'll be here," Luke answers, flipping his hat around.

There's an ache in my chest. I hadn't thought of the fact that he might already be dating someone. When he catches me watching him, it's too late to hide my confusion.

Sean clears his throat. "Here she comes, guys."

A beautiful blonde comes bouncing toward our table. She slides a beer into Sean's hand then glances at the rest of us. "So everyone *finally* decided to join you guys, huh?" Her breasts are so far out of her dress, I'm surprised I don't see nipples.

Luke's friend is our waitress?

"Yep. And we're ready to order," Sean answers, using a tone much lighter than with me earlier. I notice his eyes appraise her and want to cover them with my hands.

"How 'bout I start with you?" she says to me. "My name is Brandi, by the way. I'm your waitress, obviously."

"Obviously," I say back. She doesn't deserve my rudeness, but I'm jealous, and I'm speaking before I can stop myself. I don't know what bothers me more—Sean's gawking or the thought of Luke engaged in sweaty sex with her, but I can feel Luke watching me. So I give her my order without looking up ... not proud of my insecurity. When she's finished making her rounds, Sean orders another beer.

I lean over and whisper, "Maybe you should slow it down a

bit."

"You worry about yourself. Pretty sure I've been doing this longer than you." He takes out his phone and starts messing with it.

"Don't expect me to help if you get sick." I don't appreciate the attitude he's throwing. He's had more to drink than everybody else, which you can tell just by looking at him.

"Yeah, because that happens all the time," he says, sending someone a message.

"There's a first time for everything."

Brandi drops off my glass of cabernet while we're bickering. I take two sips before digging my own phone out of my purse. It's been buzzing for the last five minutes, and the rest of our party seems to be preoccupied with something else. I hold it in my lap and read my first missed text ... from Luke.

I don't see it.

I glance to my right, then type a quick reply before setting my phone on silent.

Don't see what?

What you see in this guy.

My hands are shaking when I reply.

He doesn't normally drink like this.

That's what they all say.

Stop texting me, or you'll get me in trouble.

I'm tired of going by the rules.

My eyes flick up to his amused ones, then I see him typing out another text.

You look gorgeous by the way.

Turning my phone face down in my lap, I do my best to fight the smile taking over my face. I feel him watching me, and nearly jump out of my chair when Sean's phone rings. He stands up and presses it to his ear. "I need to take this," he says before scurrying out of the bar.

I read the very last text.

I miss you.

Putting my phone away, I swallow the lump in my throat as Gia says something.

"Sorry, what?"

She leans forward. "I *said*: it's a good thing you two drove separately. He's on his way to alcohol poisoning." She watches me over her martini. "What's up with him?"

"I think he's stressed about work or something."

"He's a pussy," Logan retorts.

Gia makes a face at him. "*Real* mature."

I give him a dirty look. "I'm sure with this trip coming up, he's freaking out a bit. He has a lot of work he needs to catch up on." I don't mention what else is bothering him. They know he's got issues with Luke.

Speaking of Luke, he asks, "How'd it go with your mom? I heard you two talked."

It's hard to look at him, as I think of his last text. I sip my wine. "Very well, actually."

"Yeah?" He crosses his arms, the cords of his muscles flexing with the movement.

"Yeah, she seems really happy." I grin. "This may be her longest relationship since my dad." I miss this—talking about her with him. Talking about anything.

"That's good. I'm glad to hear that." He smiles genuinely, flashing his dimples, then takes off his hat and runs a hand through his sexy, mussed up hair. I try not to ogle him, but I think about how much I miss just being around him.

Gia yanks Logan out of his chair.

"What are you doin'?" he asks her.

"Come with me to the bar. I want another drink."

Luke and I watch as she tows him away.

"What was that about?"

"Hell if I know," he chuckles lightly. Silence falls between us, then he asks, "So how's everything else?"

"Good. Everything's good." I'm not sure how convincing that sounded by the way he's looking at me.

"This is weird."

"What is?"

"Everything. I want to know what you're thinking."

I swallow. "I'm thinking … I want to know why you came tonight?"

"Isn't it obvious?"

I shake my head *no*.

"Came to see you."

Chapter

REESE

Eleven

"You *do* realize I'm not going to remember this." Gia blinks after Logan tries to tell her how to defend herself. "I'm working on number three here." She points to her drink.

I'd just finished telling them about the kidnapping, before Brandi brought our meals.

"Then I'll show you tomorrow when you're sober," he replies, sliding an arm around her, planting a kiss on her cheek.

She turns to me. "Do you still have your Taser?"

"Um, yeah, though I've never used it." My eyes briefly flick to Luke's, since he's the one who bought it for me.

"I didn't know you had a Taser," Sean says, chewing. "That's cool."

"You should get her to try it on you. See if it works," Logan replies.

Gia raises a brow at him. "Would you let me try it on *you*?"

"Yeah, I'd let you."

"I find that hard to believe." She turns to me. "Anyway, how did you hear about this? On the news?"

I hold up a finger, swallowing my food. "The cab driver told me—a little old man. He picked me up in the grocery store lot where it happened."

Her eyes widen. "You took a cab here?"

"Yeah. My car was making crazy noises again. I was worried it was going to die on me, so I pulled over."

Luke and Sean both stare at me in silence.

"What?"

"You could have called one of us." Gia's forehead creases. "I would have totally picked you up."

"You'd left your phone on the counter, and I called him four or five times, but he didn't answer. Doesn't matter. At least I made it."

Sean squeezes my thigh. "Sorry babe."

"Me too," Gia says, frowning. "I'd thought I left my phone in the car. Logan and I went out to look for it earlier."

Logan takes one of her olives and pops it into his mouth. "Tell her what else we did in the car," he says, looking smug.

"Oh my gah! They don't want to hear that!" She elbows him, covering her own ears.

"Don't act like you didn't enjoy it."

"You mean all thirty seconds of it? Just shut up already. You'll embarrass yourself."

He chuckles. "It wasn't *that* fast. More like a minute."

"Oh *please*, I got gypped!"

They banter back and forth while the rest of us laugh.

"Must be nice," Sean murmurs, pointing with his fork. "Those two, going out to the car to have a quickie. Kind of gives me something to look forward to." He grins. Though his words are meant for me, they're loud enough, so the rest of our party can hear him.

"All right. Let's change the subject," I tell him nervously.

He holds up a finger. "Gia, I've got to ask you something. Maybe you can fill me in."

"Sean, you're drunk. Drop it," I plead, worried about what he'll say, but he ignores me.

"What's the deal with Reese and sex? What's she so afraid of? If anyone knows, it'd be you."

I suck in a breath, spotting Gia's horrified expression. *Oh my God, did he really just say that? How dare he bring this up.*

Luke stands in my defense, leaning over the table with nostrils flaring. "It's hardly the time or place to be discussing that. Don't you think? What the hell, man! Show her some respect."

"Luke, stop! It's okay…" It's actually not okay, but I don't want Sean's belligerence to ruin our night.

Luke stares down his target. When he's finally able to look at me, I calmly repeat, "It's okay. Sit down." It takes a moment, but he listens. I blow out a sigh of relief, but then Sean has to go and open his mouth again.

"C'mon. It's a simple fucking question. Don't even say you weren't curious about it when you dated her?"

Luke leans forward. "What part of 'shut the fuck up' don't you understand?"

"Why are you doing this?" I ask Sean, humiliated.

His expression is menacing. "Look at you, trying to be the hero," he spews at Luke with hate. "You think you're gonna win her back? I've seen the way you are staring at her. I know what you're doin'."

"Nothing wrong with looking, my *friend*. Isn't that what you said?" Luke grins mockingly. A silent message exchanges between them.

Gia murmurs, "Guys, I really don't want to get kicked out of here tonight. Can you cut the sword fight?"

"No way! I'm enjoying this," Logan retorts.

Sean pushes out of his chair, then throws some money on the table. "No problem. Enjoy what's left of your night."

"Give me your keys. I'll call you a cab." There's no way I'm letting him drive.

He digs them out of his pocket and drops them into my purse. "Don't bother." He sways. "Will's already on his way. Let's go." He scoots out my chair.

"Are you crazy? I'm not going home with you."

"Well, you're not staying here." He glares, red-faced, glancing from me, to Luke, then back to me again. I know what he's getting at, but he's gone and pissed me off, so I don't really care.

I lift my chin in defiance. "You put yourself on my shit list tonight. We will talk this over when you're *sober*. For now, I'm saying goodbye."

He presses his lips together tightly. "If you stay here—"

"You heard her," Luke calls, not letting him finish.

"Keep out of this!" I snap. When I turn back to Sean, he's halfway to the exit. I glance at the rest of the table and sigh, "This is really embarrassing."

"How could you put up with that?" Luke grumbles, sparking a fire in me.

"I didn't leave with him, did I? Thanks for your concern, but can we talk about something else?"

☆☆☆

It's been about an hour since Sean angrily stormed out, and I've been stewing over what happened—mainly the part where Luke came to my defense. It meant something to me, the way he reacted. He understands my issues with sex. He was there when

I'd nearly been raped, and felt the anger I was feeling while Sean treated me like a joke. We're still connected in that way, I guess, and once again he was there to save me.

Now that the crowd has died down, Brandi's been chatting away with him—batting her eyelashes, pushing out her breasts. I roll my eyes, watching them interact and curious about their history together.

When she'd asked what he'd been up to, he responded by saying he'd been *'enjoying the single life.'* I didn't miss the emphasis he put on the last two words either. I also didn't miss the grin he wore at the dirty look Gia had thrown him. I was probably giving him the same look. He may be an exceptional friend, but he's a pig when it comes to monogamy.

"Have you talked to Lauren lately?" Brandi asks, her big blue eyes gazing down at him.

So she knows his sister. Cute. When Luke glances at me, I pretend I'm not listening, but Gia kicks me under the table, telling me she's watching.

"A few days ago, but it was brief." He rests his head in his hands. "She'd called on her way to class—said she was checking up on me."

"You should visit her some time," she encourages. "She misses her brother."

"Yeah, I plan on it. Her moving there is the best decision she's ever made. Got her away from her asshole ex-boyfriend. I miss her, too, though."

"What'd Lauren see in that dick anyway?" Logan joins in. "Dude better run the other way if I ever see him."

"Aww ... aren't you the big, scary, tough guy?" Gia croons.

"I'm serious. I'll break his arms and legs."

"I know you are. I think it's sexy." Her voice is husky. She's a drink or two ahead of us, but it's the Long Island Iced Tea that did her in.

He leans in for a kiss. "You do?"

"Mmhmm, I do."

I want to tell them to get a room already.

"I agree with you," Brandi continues.

Doesn't she have some tables to check? My phone buzzes, so I dig it out, wondering if maybe it'll be an apology from Sean.

She's not my type, incase you're wondering. (:

My eyes flick to Luke, who's fighting a smirk. *Cocky son of a bitch.*

I don't know what you're talking about.

My phone buzzes again.

Lying doesn't become you.

My mouth drops as I read it. His assumption may be correct, but he's 100% full of himself.

A snort escapes me. *Who says I'm lying? I'm nothing like you.*

"What's so funny?" Gia asks suspiciously.

I wave it off. "I'll tell you later."

She eyes me a moment, then goes back to conversing with Brandi.

I get another text.

I see right through you. (;

Whatever. Go back to talking to Boobies... I mean Brandi.

Somebody's jealous.

Hardly.

I'd rather finish our conversation.

The conversation we barely got started.

Gia pats Logan on the shoulder. "You ready, babe? I'm getting tired."

"Let's get you home then." He takes his card back from

Brandi, and they scoot out of their chairs. He swings an arm around her to help her keep her balance.

"Do you need a ride, or are you staying?" she asks me.

I dig around for Sean's keys. "Go ahead. I'll drive his car home. But I gotta hit the ladies' room first."

"You sure you're okay to drive?"

"I'll take her if she needs a ride," Luke offers.

"I've had *two* glasses. I'm fine."

"You sure?" Gia's forehead creases.

"We've been here three hours. I stopped drinking an hour ago. I promise. I'm fine."

"Okay, see you at home then." She waves.

I turn back to Luke and Brandi, who are discussing her recent move from Flagstaff, and something about her sick mother. I tell them goodbye, not wanting to stand around like an idiot, and make my way to the restroom. When I head out to the parking lot, Luke is leaning against Sean's car, waiting for me with a devilish smirk on his face.

Chapter

REESE

Twelve

Luke takes off his hat, and his hair sticks up in every direction. It looks hot on him, of course, though I doubt he could ever look bad. "You surprised to see me?"

I bite back a smile. "Thought you were still inside, chatting it up with your *girlfriend*," I say, unlocking the car with the fob as I head toward him.

He chuckles softly. "Something you want to ask me?"

I pause, looking at him quizzically.

"Nah, that ain't your style. You'd rather jump to your own conclusions." He rubs the back of his neck, then glances at me.

"I-I don't know what you're talking about."

"Sure you don't." When I reach him, he continues, "Brandi's friends with my sister. She and Lauren were roommates up in Flagstaff, but she recently moved back to take care of her sick mother."

"*Oh*," is all I say at first. "I just assumed she was someone from your past ... maybe someone you dated."

"Would it have hurt you to ask?"

Why do I feel like I'm being scolded? "You're right. I should have asked," I admit. "I guess I figured it wasn't my business." The night air blows a gentle breeze on us, and I lean against the car beside him.

"You shouldn't be out here alone, with that killer on the loose."

"Is that why you're out here? To protect me?" I tease, knowing that's exactly what he's doing. It just comes natural for him.

"I wanted to talk to you." He tosses his hat on the hood then presses his back against the car. "You gonna tell me to go away again?"

My heart sinks a little. "No, I want to talk to you, too." I'm being pushed and pulled in so many directions. It's hard to be vulnerable with him. "Thank you for what you did earlier," I say finally, but he looks like he doesn't understand. "When Sean brought up my fear of sex—he doesn't know what happened … what almost happened. He doesn't know that you saved me back when…" I don't need to finish. "Anyway, I appreciate you keeping it to yourself." I nervously lick my lips.

"It's not my story to tell. He's lucky he walked out of here—with the way he was running his mouth. I won't hold back if there's a next time." His eyes peer down on me with conviction.

"I know," I murmur. "To be honest, it's good to see you still care."

He doesn't answer, but something else is obviously weighing on him.

"What is it?"

He hesitates. "I want to ask you somethin'."

"Okay."

"Is he pressuring you for sex?"

I inhale. "I wouldn't call it *pressuring*. It's more like insecurity about my true feelings."

"Yeah," he says, unbelieving.

"He blames himself for my not being ready. So he gets upset sometimes." I shrug. "I haven't exactly been open with him ... *that* bothers him, and I get it."

He wears an angry expression. "I don't like it."

"What guy wouldn't be insecure in his position?"

His eyes narrow, and I want to take it back.

"Okay, that was a bad response." I hold out my hands. "You and I were different. I'm going to take my foot out of my mouth now." I know I'm blushing; I can feel the heat rising in my cheeks.

"C'mon, he's manipulating you!" he growls.

"I wouldn't put up with him, if that were true," I say, folding my arms insecurely. I know Luke's just watching out for me. "We shouldn't even be talking about this."

He crosses his legs at his ankles, and glances down at me. "Why?"

"Because it's private, and it feels wrong ... like cheating in a sense. You may not have a conscience when it comes to that, but I definitely do. I'll never cheat like—"

"Me?"

"Yeah, like you." I swallow, as he looks up at the sky, a frustrated sound coming out of him. I feel like a jerk. He's only trying to help, and I can't seem to suppress my bitterness. No matter how many times I remind him it doesn't change anything. "Look, I'm sorry. I'll try not to rub it in your face anymore. I'm tired of being angry about what you did. It isn't healthy for either of us."

With a straight face, he reaches over and tucks a lock of hair behind my ear. "Apology accepted."

"I understand you're trying to be a good friend, and I

appreciate that about you."

He moves in front of me, then tilts my head back to meet his gaze.

"I've been thinking..." I feel so small when he's standing this close to me. *What was I getting ready to say?*

His mouth tips. "You've been thinking..."

Right. That's it. "I've been thinking about you and I being friends."

"Yeah?"

"Yeah." I nod slowly. "I think I'm willing to try it out for awhile. See if it works for us," I say, shrugging.

He looks amused by this. "Friends are hard to come by."

"So, what do you think?" I fidget from the way he's staring at me.

"I'm thinking I love that idea."

"Wh-what are you doing?" Warmth and electricity jolt through me when he wraps his arms around me, and murmurs into my neck.

"I'm pretty sure friends can hug."

I release a timid laugh, enjoying the feel of his body pressed against me.

"Mmm, you smell good." The vibrations of his voice send a rash of chills over my skin. "Are you cold?"

I tilt my head back and lie. "A little bit." Our eyes lock, and we're caught in some sort of trance.

His gaze drops to my lips. I'm worried he'll try to kiss me, but he presses his lips against my forehead. "I'll be the *best damn friend* you'll ever have," he whispers, rubbing his hands up and down my arms to cause some friction. He leans over and opens the car door for me. "Now get in. I don't want you catching a cold."

☆☆☆

After pulling Sean's car into his driveway, I tread toward the front door, quietly unlocking it. Will jumps off the couch, shirtless, like I startled him, the only light coming from the TV. His sandy blond hair is messed up from sleep. He looks me up and down then says, "You look nice. What are you doing here?" His voice is quiet. "Sean went to bed awhile ago."

I walk toward the kitchen, dangling Sean's keys. "Sorry if I scared you. I brought his car home. Didn't want him to have to hassle with it in the morning. Thanks for picking him up earlier, by the way."

"You're welcome." He reaches for them, and I pull back my hand.

"I'm gonna go in there and wake him up. He and I need to talk."

"I'll give him the keys in the morning. You should let him sleep it off." He follows me closely as I head for the hall, stepping over a pile of junk.

"Actually, I don't want to wait that long."

"Wait!" He rushes past me, spinning around, stretching his arms from wall to wall. When I try to get by, he blocks me.

I frown. "What's going on?"

He looks around nervously. "I don't think he should be bothered. He wasn't feeling well earlier."

"Tough titties. Why do I feel like you're hiding something?" I cross my arms, looking over his shoulder. "You're acting suspicious."

"It's not a good time," is all he says.

"Too bad. I'm going in there."

He watches me warily, but doesn't move. "Just come back

tomorrow, Reese." Now he sounds defeated.

"Look, I have no problem connecting my knee with your balls. You have three seconds to get out of my way," I threaten.

"I can't do that. Aww, fuuuckk!" He hunches over.

"I gave you fair warning." I straighten my skirt and walk past him. When I reach Sean's door, I push it open, confirming my suspicions. Clothes are strewn all over the floor. Sean lies with a naked blonde curled up beside him. Dropping his keys, I cover my mouth to muffle my cry. Tears race down both of my cheeks. How could this happen to me again? I'm not sure whether to scream or walk away with my dignity, but I certainly don't want to look back.

"I tried to stop you," Will says, standing behind me.

I turn around, darting out of the room. "They can have each other. Tell him to lose my number. In fact, tell him to find another place to live. I don't want to see him again. God, I'm just like my mother!"

"You're what?"

"I'm thinking out loud!" I yell, bolting for the door.

He follows me. "For what it's worth ... I'm sorry."

I don't answer. I'm too overwhelmed to come up with a response. It's hard to explain my emotions—anger, confusion, embarrassment, relief. I slam the door and hold back a sob as I hurry my way home.

Chapter
REESE
Thirteen

"You're coming to Vegas. There's no backing out," Gia demands through the phone. She and Logan arrived in Vegas a couple hours ago. She's been going on and on about their room, and how Logan already won two thousand dollars on a slot machine at Bally's.

I pop a cheesecake bite into my mouth. I've probably eaten about ten of them, all in the course of fifteen minutes. "It just doesn't sound appealing anymore. I've got the whole house to myself. Maybe I'll just lay in bed and figure out why men can't stay faithful to me."

"No way! Those plane tickets are non-refundable. Remember? You won't be able to get your money back. Plus, it'll be the perfect post break-up getaway. What about all our plans?" Her voice has turned whiney. "If you don't go, you're going to regret it and get depressed."

"I already *am* depressed," I say, frowning at the empty container, realizing I've eaten the last bite of cheesecake. I'd consider buying more, but my stomach is starting to hurt.

"C'mon Reese! I want you to come. Tell you what ... if you have a miserable time, you can fly home early, and I promise not to bug you about it."

I lie on the couch and throw my feet up, closing my eyes. I'm not sure I believe her.

"I thought you wanted to stay clear of Sean."

"I do."

"What are the chances you're going to run into each other if you're home all week?"

She's right. I've ignored his persistent phone calls and shut all the windows and blinds, but he's already come by the house a few times. "I guess you have a point," I say, groaning.

"Does this mean you're coming?"

Silently weighing my options, I'm not thrilled about it being just the three of us, and having to deal with their constant PDA — sort of like following a couple on their honeymoon. I *will* have my own room, though, and my chances of running into Sean are then non-existent. *That* idea alone trumps everything else. Rolling my eyes, I decide to give in. "*Okay*, I'll go."

She squeals so loud I have to pull the phone away. "We're going to have so much fun! Reese is coming!" she yells to Logan, and he mutters something back. "I better let you go now. He's giving me dirty looks and wants to go gamble. Love you! See you tomorrow."

We say our goodbyes, then I turn off my phone again.

☆☆☆

Bang, bang, bang. "You're going to have to talk to me, Reese. I know you're in there. The cab just pulled up."

It's the fourth time he's come over in the last forty-eight hours, but the first time he'll get a response. "Go away!" I tell him, peeking through the peephole. When he doesn't move, I realize I'll soon be face-to-face with the cheating bastard. I've got a flight to catch, and I'll be *damned* if he makes me miss it. Vegas is starting to sound better every second, especially with him standing outside my door.

"She was in the car when he picked me up. He'd had some friends over that night," he says loudly enough so I can hear him.

I press my forehead to the door and close my eyes.

"Are you there?"

"Please, just go," I say quietly.

"I never touched her before then. I swear I never—"

"Look Sean, I'm not asking for an explanation. I'm asking you to leave." Taking another peek, I notice how tired he looks. He's got his hands jammed in his pockets, and he drops his head, letting out a sigh.

"Would you hear me out for a minute?"

I check the time, resigning. My eyes take a quick sweep around the house, making sure all the lights are off. Grabbing my stuff, I swing open the door, then bump him with my suitcase, pushing past him.

He wraps his hand around my wrist to stop me. "Wait…" His voice is desperate. When I turn to face him, his eyes take their time roaming over my short yellow sundress that ties around the neck. "You look nice. Is that new?"

"Are you serious? Let go of me!"

"I'm sorry I hurt you. I never intended for us to go down this way. I was completely shitfaced and—"

"You clearly let me know your intentions at the restaurant. Now let go of my arm, *please*." I try to yank it back, but he tightens his grip.

"It's not about the sex, dammit! It's about you and me. You're never going to be ready."

I glare at him.

"Shit! That came out wrong," he says, rubbing his free hand over his face. "Fuck! If I thought you and I had a chance, I wouldn't have touched her."

"What the hell are you talking about?"

"*Him*!" he yells, pointing toward Luke's house. "I saw the way you looked at him, that night at the restaurant; not once have you looked at me like that. You're still in love with him!"

My heart rate picks up, and I break away. "You're delusional, Sean." I rush toward the cab, wanting to get as far from him as possible.

"That's all you have to say? Tell me you're not in love with him!" he shouts over

my shoulder. "You can't even say it."

I brush a single tear off my face—because I'm angry, because he's right. I *know* he's right. I had jumped into another relationship, but I hadn't been ready. I've been wracking my brain for two days, realizing my mistake, but it doesn't excuse him for what he did. It doesn't make it okay. I slide into the back of the yellow taxi, shutting the door without replying, and tell the driver where to take me. We pull out of the driveway, and I'm a mixture of emotions, but mostly I feel relief.

☆☆☆

I watch the passengers line up to board the plane, finishing up my second cocktail at a bar outside my gate. I feel the liquor working it's magic. I haven't stood up since I started, but I can tell I already have a good buzz. The bartender went a little generous on the vodka, and it all just sort of snuck up on me, while I've been sitting here mulling over what Sean said to me earlier.

There's no way I'll let him shame me for my feelings. I tried to love him, tried to make it work. I wouldn't have cheated, even if I knew we were headed toward a dead end. I'd unintentionally led him on, thinking time would make us stronger, but we should've broken up a long time ago. Regardless, my shoulders feel lighter. This trip will probably do some good for me.

After taking care of my tab, I blow out a long, slow breath, then make my way to the end of the line. When I finally reach the podium, I hand a tall, short-haired woman my boarding pass. Her name is Lynn. She scans it with a curious expression, as her glasses slide down to the tip of her nose.

"Reese Johnson?"

"Yes," I smile politely.

"It looks like your seat has been upgraded to first class."

My gaze falls on the ticket then back to her. "That's got to be a mistake. I didn't pay for first class."

She presses her finger to the computer screen. "Nope. It says it right here. No mistake. Today must be your lucky day!" Her eyes twinkle.

"Wow ... okay." I don't really know what to say. So I stand there with a dumb look on my face, before she tells me where to go, shooing me forward. I walk through the gate in a daze, but excited. Gia had to have been behind this. I wonder how much she paid.

When I step inside the plane, I scan the seats, finding mine three rows back, next to the window. The seat beside it is empty, but I doubt I'll have the whole row to myself. The plane is nearly full, and we still have close to five minutes before departure ... and that's if we leave on time. I lift my overstuffed suitcase, shoving it into the bin above me, then slide into the leather seat. I definitely see the difference. It's more inviting with triple the room. There are only two seats compared to the normal three. I can't decide if I want to take a nap, or enjoy all the luxuries that first class will bring me.

Laying my head back, I close my eyes, inhaling through my nose, and hope this is a sign that things will get better from this moment. A familiar soapy scent awakens my senses, causing goose bumps to rise up the back of my neck.

"Dreaming about me?"

Chapter
REESE
Fourteen

I flick my eyes open and straighten in my seat. Luke sits beside me, wearing a ball cap and a grin the size of Texas. He holds what looks to be a beer in a plastic cup. With his gaze sweeping over me, he fingers the hemline of my dress. "I like this. Yellow suits you."

"Wha-what are you doing here?" I ask, placing my palm over my chest.

"Going to Vegas," he answers matter-of-factly.

"Well, *yeah*, but I hadn't heard anything about it. Why didn't you tell me?" Not that I don't want him to go. I'm thrilled, but just surprised.

He shrugs casually. "Sort of decided last minute."

"Do Logan and Gia know?"

"Yeah." He finishes all that's in his cup, then crushes the plastic.

"Why didn't you tell me?"

"You asked that already." He squints.

"Oh yeah. I forgot."

He scrutinizes me, and I wonder if he's about to mention my break up. Logan had told him the other day when Luke dropped my car off at the shop. He'd come by to pick up my keys when I was holed up in my bedroom. Another thought comes to me.

"Wait … did you do this?" I point to my seat.

His gaze lingers, then he leans in to inhale me, his breath tickling my neck.

"What are you doing?" I squirm. He grins lazily, and I have to cross my legs. The alcohol intensifies my body's reaction to him.

"You been drinkin'?"

"You didn't answer me."

"You first."

"I had two cocktails," I relent.

"Why was that hard for you?"

"It wasn't." I glance at him, and a loud voice comes over the speaker, telling us the time we should expect to arrive in Vegas, and the conditions of the skies. I'm relieved to learn the weather will be cooler than the triple digits in Phoenix, though it's only by seven or eight degrees. A moment later we're taxiing the runway.

"I'd meant to get a small buzz, but the bartender forgot to add the cranberry. I feel like I've downed a whole bottle of vodka, and need to get something to eat. How'd you manage to get that?"

His eyes drop to the crumpled mess that was his cup, then he stuffs it in the pocket of the seat in front of him. "I uh … had a stewardess sneak it to me before take off."

"You couldn't get one at the airport?"

"Didn't have time."

I arch a brow. "So what? You hypnotized her with your charm, and she readily handed it over? Just like that?"

"Hypnotized her with my charm?"

"Yeah."

"I don't like to fly," he offers flatly.

"*Oooh.*" Why didn't I know that? "I guess that's something you and Gia have in common."

He doesn't say anything, and I'm reminded of our earlier conversation.

"How much do I owe you?"

His eyes are questioning.

"For my seat. You obviously paid for this."

"I'm not taking your money, princess." He stretches out his legs and flips his hat around backwards.

"C'mon, tell me."

He shakes his head. "We're friends. Consider it a gift."

There isn't a point in arguing. No matter how much I beg, it won't change things. "Thank you."

"Don't worry about it. Your drooling I can handle—"

I bump his shoulder. "I do *not* drool!"

"I beg to differ."

The force from the speed of the plane has us grabbing our armrests. Our skin brushes together, then that familiar charge shoots between us. I glance at his face. You wouldn't know by looking at him, but I can sense his fear moving through me. We start to lift off, and he intertwines our fingers.

"Are you okay?" I never imagined him being afraid of anything. He nods, but I don't believe him. After awhile, the plane begins to level, and he releases my hand. I instantly miss the connection, placing mine in my lap.

Over thirty minutes in the air, and Luke's nerves are long gone. He's ordered a couple more beers, while I've snacked on pita chips and hummus. If I consumed any more alcohol, he'd have to carry me out of here. Plus, I don't want to tire out before we get to Vegas. I plan on having fun tonight, but there's something that's been bothering me since he showed up here.

"So let's get rid of the elephant in the room. Why haven't you asked me about Sean yet? I know that Logan told you." I pretend not to notice how the sides of our thighs are pressed together, or the way his arm brushes mine every so often. If I want to take our friendship seriously, I'll need to get used to this, without getting flustered.

"Figured you'd bring it up when you were ready." He shrugs, gazing at me. "I actually expected you to be more upset."

I sigh. "I am—was—upset. It's hard to explain. In some ways I feel like a weight has been lifted. Deep down I knew we were headed for it. Our relationship had been rocky for a while. I just didn't expect things to end the way they did. If that even makes sense?"

"Sure," he shrugs.

"So I think it's time I give up on men—maybe become a nun," I say, shoving a chip into my mouth.

His eyes dance. "A nun?" He chuckles softly.

"Not literally, you dope. I used to be independent and content with my life back when I was single. I want to be that girl again ... the *old* me."

Playfully tugging on a strand of my hair, he says, "You *are* the same girl." We experience some turbulence, and his hand covers mine for the second time. His eyes slide over. "Sorry, I'm a pussy."

"A lot of people share a fear of flying."

"I usually keep that detail to myself." His mouth tips. "So what's your excuse for drinkin' a bottle of vodka so early?" he teases.

"It's sort of a long story." And I'm not sure he wants to hear it.

His tongue darts out to wet his lips, and I follow the movement.

"I like listening to you talk."

Stop thinking about those lips! Stop thinking about that tongue!

I meet his eyes, realizing he caught me staring, then let out a steady breath. "I ran into Sean today. I hadn't seen him since that night." He nods, encouraging me to go on. "He told me why he did it. Why he slept with that woman. I'm not giving him an excuse, but ... in a way I understand him."

"You understand him?" he asks, bunching his forehead. "What the fuck is there to understand?"

Okay, he's angry. How can I explain this? "There are things that—"

"What did he say to you?" he interrupts.

There's no way I'm letting him know my feelings for him played a major part in it. Fidgeting from my nerves, I tell him, "That's not important. What I realize is I may have been partially to blame for him making that decision. It's not that I'm completely holding myself responsible." I hold out my hands, before continuing, "I'm just—"

"Sticking up for him," he snorts, rubbing his jaw as it tenses.

I shake my head. "Let me explain before you get all upset."

"You don't have to. I can see where you're going with this."

"What he did was wrong. I completely agree. I also know I'd been hurting him unintentionally for quite some time."

"So he got you to feel sorry for him." He chuckles sardonically. "I'm gonna shoot it to you straight, Reese. You weren't giving him what he wanted, so the prick went and found somewhere else to stick his dick."

My mouth drops from the shock of his words, and I'm bursting with rage. *How dare he say that to me after all he put me through!* "No, Luke, that's what *you* did!" I point, making him flinch, then a voice comes over the speaker, telling us to prepare for landing, but I'm not finished. "You left and cheated on me — told me to trust you, then went off to marry another woman! I've never been so betrayed in all my life." I try not to cry. "Maybe you should keep your opinions regarding my relationships to yourself. You hardly have the right." I should have never brought it up in the first place. I had opened up to him as a friend but wasn't expecting he'd respond so rudely.

Grabbing the armrests, he clenches tightly, looking angry instead of afraid. We land, then roll down the runway. With eyes filled with fury, he moves an inch from my face. I can smell a hint of mint and alcohol on his breath while he debates what he's going to say. When the plane comes to a stop, he asks, "You want the truth?"

Rows of people start exiting the plane. My breathing shallows from the

expression that shows on his face. "That's all I've wanted."

His nostrils flare. "The last woman I touched was you — only you. So stop pointing your little finger, unless you want to point it at yourself!"

I shake my head, not understanding.

He stands at his full height, then reaches into the bin above me to grab both of our bags. His arms flex as he walks right off the plane with one in each hand.

"Wait!" I stand, racing to catch up with him, but he's already through the gate. I find him inside the airport, waiting, our bags beside him on the floor. "Why would you say that?" I ask once I'm close to him.

Stepping toward me, he places his hands on either side of my face, searching my eyes. Without warning, he crashes his lips to mine, hard and demanding. I gasp, and my insides come alive, at war with myself for enjoying this. He releases me before I can protest. His chest heaves as he tastes me on his lips. My heart thunders violently, and I try to catch my breath. "I was never married, Reese." Grabbing our bags, he strides away, leaving me in a trance.

Chapter
LUKE
Fifteen

"You can't just say that and walk off!" she yells from behind me.

I smirk at her distress. I couldn't help leaving her hanging the way I did. I'm tired of her saying that I'd cheated—that I'd betrayed her. It pisses me off that she'd think so low of me, and to top it off, stick up for Sean after what he did. That dick will get what's coming to him. I made a promise, and I plan to keep it.

She runs her mouth, following after me. "What do you mean you were never married, Luke? Talk to me!"

I spin around, walking backward. "I *mean* I wasn't married—never touched the woman."

Her face is incredulous. "But I met her! Saw her two or three times! At the hospital, she—"

"Things aren't always what they seem." I stop at the exit, peering down on her, then hold the door open. She marches through with a scowl on her face, brushing my chest with her shoulder, then waits for me to lead her toward the cab line. If she thinks this attitude is going to get her what she wants, she's setting herself up for disappointment. When I check to see if she's following, I notice her eyes are watering. *Shit ...* I don't do well with crying women, never have. Plus, I'm dealing with my own emotions—one minute feeling sorry for her, the next I'm pissed off. If it weren't for her lack of trust in me, we wouldn't be in this mess. The thought of that prick putting his hands on her nearly pushes me over the edge. The only thing worse is the repeat visual in my head, of her enjoying it.

"This isn't funny," she chokes.

Lifting her chin with my finger and thumb, I force her to meet my gaze. "You and I are gonna talk. All right?"

She rolls her eyes in attempt to control her tears. "My heart's pounding like crazy. I'm so confused." She sniffs.

"We need privacy. I'll fill you as soon as we have it."

She nods in understanding, and then it's our turn to get in a cab. Grabbing our bags, I toss them in the trunk, giving orders to the driver. Traffic is slow, and we arrive at The Cosmopolitan an hour later. We're greeted by the bellman in front of the entrance. I hand over our bags, then shoot Logan a text, letting him know of our arrival. This is her first time in Vegas and my first time at The Cosmopolitan.

"Wow," Reese says, taking it all in as we make our way to the reservation desk. "Look at all the crystal chandeliers. I've never seen anything like it."

"Aren't you girls the ones who picked it out?"

"Yeah, but in person it's even better than the pictures."

I'll take her anywhere she wants, if it'll get the same reaction.

Moments later, we're all checked in, and Reese turns around to face me. "Are we going to do this in my room? I don't want to wait any longer."

I nod. "Your room is fine." Shit, I'm nervous, wondering how's she'll react once I finally tell her the truth. She'll probably hate me more than before. I unfold the map the concierge gave me, and we find the closest elevators, moving toward them. Placing my hand on the small of her back, I urge her in front of me, getting a nice view of her ass. When she flicks her gaze over her shoulder, I don't bother hiding it. Her eyes narrow, and I smirk.

We reach the elevators, and Reese presses the UP button. Three dudes who look to be in their mid-twenties step in behind us, pressing their floor number. The doors slide closed, and my phone chimes loudly in my pocket.

"Bet it's Logan," Reese murmurs. I pull it out and take a quick glance at the screen.

Cool. Meet us at the pool once you're settled.

Tapping my reply, I lift my head, noticing the tall guy in the corner appreciating Reese's curves. He meets my eyes, and I stare him down, straightening my shoulders. *That's right, punk. She's mine.* Moving my arm around her, I grip her waist and pull her against me. She squirms out of my reach, like this bothers her, and the three of them snicker with their eyes aimed at the floor.

"Somethin' funny?" I ask, not knowing who I'm angrier with—The Three Stooges or Reese.

"Nah, we're cool, man," says the guy in the middle with short, spiky hair. The other two don't speak, and they're no longer laughing. We come to a stop, and they all shuffle out when the door opens. Reese prances to the other side of the elevator, and I crack my neck to relieve some tension.

She turns around to face me. "What makes you think you can touch me like that? I thought we agreed to be friends."

Flipping my hat backward, I ask, "Did you want me to set you up with one of them? Is that it?"

"You *know* that's not what it is," she points. "You were having some sort of pissing contest!"

"I didn't like the way that dude was looking at you."

"You were looking at my ass two minutes before!" she says, raising her voice, now even more irritated.

"That's different!"

"Oh yeah? How so?"

"I'm allowed to look at your ass!"

"Says who?"

"Says me!" I say, wanting to shake her and bury myself inside her at the same time.

Her face reddens. "You still have explaining to do. I don't even know if I believe you. You can't just kiss me, claim me as yours, and act as if the past never happened!"

"Judging by your reaction, sweetheart, you enjoyed that kiss as much as I did! You're not fooling anybody."

Her eyes fill with fire. "You are *so* wrong. I hated it!"

I stride toward her 'til I'm inches from her face. She steps back, hitting the wall behind her. She lifts her chin in defiance when I move closer, and I dip my head so we're nose to nose, inhaling her flowery scent. "Liar," I whisper. Grabbing her hand, I place it flat over my chest. Her breathing falters, but she keeps it there. Goose bumps trickle along her skin. My eyes journey over her mouth, down the rise and fall of her breasts, to the hardening of her nipples.

"Do you feel that? That's my heart beating for you. It knows who I belong to."

She releases short breaths, the struggle clear in her eyes.

"Your lips call for me to taste them. Your nipples ache for my touch." I tilt my head. "You can deny it all you want, but your body tells me differently. You want to fight it … I'll respect your wishes. I won't touch you again until you beg me to. *And you will beg me."* The door slides open, and I walk out of the elevator, leaving her panting.

"You are way too full of yourself, mister," she yells, marching angrily behind me.

I may have been bluffing, but she'd gone and pissed me off, lying about hating the kiss, squirming away from me like she did. Knowing that kiss might have been our last feels like a hard blow to the chest. "You bring it out of me," I tell her, slowing my pace, allowing her to catch up with me.

We find her room at the end of the hall, and she swipes her key in the door. As soon as it unlatches, she grips the center of my shirt, pulling me in with her.

"Start talking," she says, releasing me.

I get lost in her big green eyes. Moments of our history flash through my mind. "You want to take the couch?" I point her toward the loveseat. We walk over and take a seat, then she waits for me to say something, but suddenly I'm nervous. "I don't know where to start."

"Let's start with the wife," her voice is quiet. "Tell me who she is."

I blow out a breath, tossing my hat on the table. "She's a friend … and I swear I never touched her. She sort of had a thing for me. Maybe she said what she did to fuck with me. I don't know."

She raises a questioning brow. *"Okay.* Is she an old friend or a new friend?"

"New," I say, rubbing the back of my neck. "I met her after I left."

"She's an awfully pretty friend," she says, suspicious.

"Doesn't matter. The only woman I see is you."

"That's smooth."

"It's the truth." She waits for me to continue, but I don't.

"Where'd you meet her?"

"In the middle of a sting operation involving Glenn Ryann. Rachelle's an FBI agent. She was working undercover as an escort."

Her eyes widen, and she gasps. "Your father? Why would you go anywhere near that man?"

"I ran out of options. The calls started coming when he got out of prison, then every other week turned into every other day, then twice a day. You get where I'm goin' with this," I say, resting my elbows on my knees. "When I ignored him, he'd move on to Lauren. It was an endless cycle."

"What did he want?"

"Wanted me to pay back what I owed him. In his mind, it was my fault he'd been arrested. I'd been the one to turn him in."

She looks horrified. "What did he expect you to do? You were a child! And he committed those crimes."

"Anything he asked. Money. Time." I look at her. "Said I'd have a target on my head until I was all paid up."

"Couldn't you go to the cops?"

I snort. "Money changes people, Reese. I didn't know who to trust. I told you, my father had people in law enforcement working for him."

"How much did he ask you to pay?"

"It wasn't just about the money with him. He wanted me to suffer—wanted to watch me go against everything I believe in, do things I'd promised to never be a part of."

"He wanted to break you."

I nod, and her eyes soften.

"What did you tell him?"

"Told him to leave me the fuck alone," I growl. "Told him to stop harassing Lauren."

"But it didn't work?" she asks, folding her hands in her lap.

"Nah, he just changed his approach. Started threatening to hurt the people I love. Like I told you, everyone I care about gets hurt. I couldn't allow that to happen again." She touches my shoulder, and I gaze deep into her eyes, letting her know the seriousness of it. "He killed my mom in that fire, Reese. He admitted it."

She shakes her head, her hair spilling over her shoulders, tears filling her eyes. "I'm so sorry. I had no idea what you were going through. No idea."

"The hardest part is knowing things would be different, if I'd been there, if I hadn't gone with him that day."

"It isn't your fault, Luke," she chokes on her words.

"Don't do that." I use my thumb to wipe the tears rolling down her face. "I don't like to see you cry."

"I'm trying. I still have so many questions." She inhales, flattening her palms on her knees. "The last night you came to see me. You were hurt. Your eyes looked haunted. What happened to you then?"

I pause, thinking of how to word it, not wanting to freak her out. "I'd gotten into a fight with one of Glenn's men. It was messy." Too messy to get into with her right now. She looks satisfied by my explanation.

"Why didn't you tell me the truth from the beginning?"

"You would've tried to stop me. You would've gotten involved."

She squints, chewing on her lip. "I don't know. Maybe—"

Rubbing my hands over my face, I say, "C'mon. No matter what I'd asked, or what you'd promised, you would've gotten involved. And I sure as *hell* wasn't gonna risk it. You could've been hurt or *worse*."

She's usually not one to give up so easily, but she doesn't argue. "So where does the FBI come into this? Where's your father? How'd you get out?"

I clench my fists. How the hell am I going to do this?

She senses my hesitation. "What is it?"

"Give me a minute," I say, standing, feeling my palms sweat. I start pacing the room. "What I'm about to tell you ... you aren't gonna like. I need you to let me explain though."

"*Okay*," she says tentatively. When I stop and face her, she's standing.

There's no easy way to say this. I pinch the bridge of my nose. "The Feds were involved from the beginning. So was the DEA." My eyes flick to hers, and she nods, waiting. "After Glenn made his threats, I didn't know who to turn to, but then Andrew came to mind. He'd done side jobs with private detectives. He was a former cop. It made sense to go to him." I look at her again and see the pain in her expression, clasping my hands over my head.

Her hands shake when she covers her mouth. "My ... my father? You got my father involved?"

"I didn't know what else to do."

"But you *knew* it was dangerous." She works it over in her head. "The day he died, you were there in the hospital. I'd learned about your wife. She came in and asked the nurse for your room number."

My jaw clenches. "Damn it! She was never my wife," I growl.

"No, I know that. I believe you. Wh-why were you at the hospital?" she asks, gripping the back of a chair for balance. "My God, were you shot?" I nod, and she closes her eyes. "My father died in a shootout. They ... they said he was working undercover. Were you there? Were you with him?"

I can't look at her anymore, and my voice cracks, "Yes."

A sob escapes her lips. When she hunches over, I try to hold her. "Don't!" She holds out her hand to stop me. "You lied to me; both of you did!"

"Only to protect you."

Shaking her head with a look of shock, she says, "He's dead because you brought him into this."

I don't deny it. "I'm sorry. Every second of every day, I'm sorry. I know it's not enough."

Her eyes are aimed at the floor. "I ... I need some time to process this. I don't even know what to say." Wiping her tears, she reaches for her purse.

"Stay. I'll go."

She shakes her head, and there's a knock at the door. The bellboy walks in with our suitcases, glancing at us uncomfortably. I give him a twenty, and he leaves.

"I'm going to take a walk, check out the casino," she says with her back to me. "I need to be alone for awhile."

"He wasn't supposed to be there." I swallow.

"I can't right now, Luke. We'll finish this later." She walks out the door, and I stand there with a broken heart, watching her leave.

Chapter

REESE

Sixteen

I'd left Luke alone in my hotel room, unsure what to even say to him. Did he expect me to forgive him, when he and my father had been lying all that time? Why would he involve him, knowing how risky it'd been? He should have come to me first, out of simple respect. Instead they'd plotted behind my back. And they did it together. I'm furious with both of them. Of course, I can't blame Luke entirely. My father was a grown man ... and he was stubborn; it probably wouldn't have mattered if I'd demanded him not to get involved. He would've done it regardless. Either way, they should've told me. I don't care what their intentions were. I'm without a father because of it.

"Sorry," I say, running into a group of women who are dressed to the nines, not really paying attention. They grant me a few dirty looks, then continue on their way, disregarding me. Maybe taking a walk wasn't the best idea. My eyes narrow on an empty row of slot machines. I've never gambled before, but I figure the slots are a good place to start. Picking the one on the end, I take a seat, loading it with some money, hoping it'll last since I'm only betting quarters. I stay clear of the MAX BET button just to be safe, pressing the BET ONE instead, watching the bars and cherries spin.

Thoughts continue to play in my head. *'He wasn't supposed to be there,'* Luke had said, referring to my father. What had he meant by that? And if that were true, why had he been there? How much time had they spent together? Was it possible they had become friends? What role had my father played in all of it? All of these questions and Luke has all the answers. Suddenly I'm brought back to a conversation I'd had with my dad. It had been right before he'd left. He'd been encouraging my relationship with Luke. "Hold on to him," he'd said. "Good things come to those who wait."

The words had thrown me for a loop. In the past, my father had never liked him—told me to stay far away from him. Of course I'd been a little girl then. When I'd brought it up years later, he'd confessed that he didn't mean it, saying he was jealous—that Luke had been more of a man than he had been. In the end, he'd been grateful that Luke had protected me—not only from his drunken abuse, but the night I'd nearly been raped. My father had been in prison then, but Luke swooped in like a dark angel, saving me before it could happen. The memory puts a sick feeling low in my gut. That day could've turned out so much worse. Shaking the thought from my memory, going back to my father, if I want to get to the bottom of this, there's only one person who has the answers. I just hope I'm strong enough to deal. It's a lot to take in, but deep down I know I need the closure.

After losing forty bucks, I decide to give up rather than gamble away any more money. Draining my wallet within the first couple hours of being in Vegas probably isn't the best idea. Hopefully later I'll have better luck. I head to the restroom and splash some water on my face, more thankful than ever for waterproof mascara. *Man up, Reese. Get control of your emotions.* I inhale, then blow out a breath. Besides the blotchiness, no one would be able to tell I'd been crying.

My mission is to go down to the pool, find Gia, and rip her a new one. I have a feeling her leaving me in the dark about our extra vacationer wasn't much of an accident. She was probably worried I wouldn't have come, although I'd informed her that Luke and I had patched things up a few days ago. Maybe she thought it wasn't important enough to mention.

Cocktail waitresses, dressed in denim, scurry their way around the crowds, serving drinks and taking orders. Loud music booms over the speakers. Belligerent, swimsuit-clad men and women, with glazed eyes, grind on each other. I circle the pool, searching for a hot pink bikini, figuring it'll be easier to single her out that way. My eyes drift to the rows of royal blue lounge chairs lining the water, and then I spot her, lying on a chair, facing the sun with no sign of Logan. Slipping off my sandals, I dip my feet into the cool water, then make my way toward her, taking the empty chair beside her.

"That was quick." She stretches out her hand, like she's waiting for me to give her something. I'm not able to see behind her shades, but I'm guessing her eyes are closed.

"I've got a question. Why didn't you tell me Luke was coming?"

Startled, her head lifts, and a slow smirk crawls onto her face. "Hey you! I totally thought you were Logan." She looks me over. "What took you so long? And why aren't you wearing a suit?"

"I got a little sidetracked. Are you going to answer me, or are you purposely avoiding the question?" I narrow my eyes.

"About Luke? I just found out yesterday. I've been busy. I

guess it slipped my mind."

I don't see anything in her expression that would lead me to believe she isn't telling the truth. I obviously have some trust issues to work through.

"Are you upset he's here?"

"I don't know what I am honestly."

"I thought things were cool between the two of you. Has something changed since then?"

I'm not about to get into *that*; not now at least. I don't want her skewed opinions on the situation affecting my own. I need to have all the facts first. And I certainly don't want whatever drama ensues between us to ruin their vacation. "Well, I ... sort of ran into Sean today, right before I left. Add my lack of sleep to the mix, and the surprise of seeing Luke at the airport, and apparently it's a recipe for turning me into a bitch."

She places her shades on top of her head, scowling. "Why am I not surprised Sean had something to do with it? I *knew* you wouldn't be able to escape the cheating bastard! Let me guess. He begged for you to take him back?"

"Not exactly. He knows I'm done with him." *Though he sent me a couple texts earlier, and I haven't responded.*

"Then what did he want?"

"He wanted me to understand why it happened. It was like he was justifying his actions or something."

"Please tell me your joking," she grumbles.

"*No*, I'm afraid not."

"So what were his reasons? The skank fell from the sky and miraculously landed on his dick?"

I shake my head, almost laughing. In truth, Gia seems more upset about this than I am. I probably shouldn't have brought it up. Sean is a tiny dot on the spectrum compared to the other thoughts swirling around in my head.

"You know what?" I say, slapping my hands on my knees. "I don't want to waste any more time talking about him. This is supposed to be our vacation. I'm over it."

She grins, sliding her shades back on. "That's right. Forget him! I like that idea. There are so many other men we could discuss," she says, tipping her head toward the pool. I look over, spotting a group of guys close to our age, standing in a circle. They all pass glances our way, and one of them winks when he catches me watching. I quickly dart my eyes away.

And on *that* note, I look over my shoulders. "Where's Logan anyway?"

She shrugs. "Hell if I know. They're supposed to be getting drinks, but that was a while ago. The line must be long. Aren't you going to swim?"

I didn't miss the, *'they're'* in her answer, and I really don't want to face Luke yet. "Actually, I still want to check out the rest of the casino. Plus, I was thinking about buying a new swimsuit today." That much is true.

"Normally I would protest, but I do realize I'm lucky I got you to come in the first place. You'll still go shopping with me later, right?"

"Of course. And you said you planned on lying out by the pool every day. It's not like I'm gonna miss out. I'll be here tomorrow and the next."

"Yeah, that's fine. There are a couple other pools that are a little more relaxed, less partying. By the way, what did you think of the rooms? Nice, aren't they?"

I nod. "And *huge*." I hadn't really gotten a chance to look at all of it, but from what I'd seen, they're pretty fancy.

"Just wait until tonight, when the entire strip is lit up. You're gonna love it." Readjusting in her chair, she turns on her stomach, picking her bikini bottoms out of her butt.

My eyes widen when I see her backside. "Crap, Gia! You're fried! How long have you been out here?"

"Since about nine-thirty or ten. I fell asleep on my stomach earlier," her voice is muffled from the chair.

"You should probably roll back over."

"I'm not too worried about it. It'll be tan by morning. I'll roll over in a few minutes."

I hope she's right, or she's going to be hurting. "Don't fall asleep again."

"I won't ... Oh!" She snaps, lifting her head. "We made reservations at The Blue Ribbon Sushi Bar. We're supposed to be there by six. It'd be fun to dress up again."

"Tonight?" My forehead bunches.

She frowns at my expression. "No. Tomorrow night. Is that okay?"

"Yeah ... I ... I'm just thinking about what I'll wear." The lie slips out, and thankfully she accepts it.

"I packed my whole closet, if you're worried about it. You can borrow something of mine. Logan and I are right next door. Tonight we could cruise the strip, maybe do a little gambling. What do you think?" she asks, shielding her eyes from the sun.

"I think it sounds fun." I add a bit of enthusiasm to my voice. "I better get going while I still have time to shop."

"'K, good luck!" She waves. "See you soon."

Waving back, I slam into Logan as soon as I turn. Pushing my hands off of his hard, chiseled chest, I cause his drinks to spill over. "Ahhh!" is all that comes out of my mouth.

He grins crookedly. "Sorry to disappoint you, ma'am, but I'm taken. However, my *friend* over here is a stud, and he might be willing to help you." He tips his head in Luke's direction, and my eyes betray me, drifting over all the planes and valleys that make up Luke's body. There's not a male in this place who could ever compete with the god-like creature standing in front of me. Damn! Why does he have to look so damn perfect? It helps him get away with things he should not be able to get away with. He stares right back at me, but if he noticed me checking him out, it doesn't show. Swallowing the knot in my throat, I take one more sweep of his body then force myself to look away.

"I hope you've got a suit on underneath that," Logan says to me, planting a chaste kiss on Gia's lips.

"She's not going to swim with us," Gia answers. "She isn't staying."

Luke strides away without saying a word. Everything about him looks tense.

"What's wrong with him?" Gia asks.

Logan shrugs, digging a bottle of sunscreen out of her bag, then points it at her, spraying.

She yelps. "What the hell are you doing?"

"You're all red. You need it." He continues to spray her while she protests. "Move your hands."

"I'm taking Logan's side on this," I say, putting in my own two cents.

"Grrr … fine!" she relents, letting him finish spraying her. "Seriously guys. I never burn."

When he's finished, he turns the spray on himself, then frowns at me. "So why aren't you swimming with us?"

"I'll swim tomorrow. I want to check out the rest of the casino and maybe do a little shopping while I'm at it."

He sips on a beer, climbing into the chair I'd just been sitting in. "You hit any slots yet?"

"About an hour ago." I swing my thumb toward the casino. "Lost forty bucks pretty quickly. I'm not sure what the big deal is on gambling. I didn't really enjoy it." Of course there were other things that may have prevented me from having a good time.

"Yeah ...we'll see what you think after you win."

I let out a long sigh. "All right. I guess I'm gonna get going."

"See ya." Gia waves. "Good luck finding a suit."

Logan raises his hand in the form of a salute, then I take the path back toward the casino, seeing no sign of Luke.

Chapter

REESE

Seventeen

I purchased two bikinis yesterday within the first hour of shopping, then went back to my hotel room to get ready for the night. The events of the day had exhausted me, and I fell asleep pretty quickly by the end of it, only to be woken up a few times by my cell phone. Sean must have a screw loose if he thinks I'd give him a second chance, but judging by his messages he's dealing with some serious regrets. There's this guilt that's been festering in my soul, for letting things go as far as they went with him.

The four of us tried out the Boulevard pool today, where we rented a cabana. Other than a few clipped words here and there, Luke and I didn't speak. He'd given me my space, and I'd been appreciative for it. Last night, when we'd all walked the strip, we were both somber, keeping our distance. Whenever Gia brought up our quiet demeanor, we'd seemed to be on the same page, just shrugging it off, pretending to be oblivious.

We'd spent nearly all day at the pool, with nothing resolved, but the air was different between us. Several times our eyes would lock, and the heat of his gaze had sparked a fire within me, causing several moments of awkwardness. An accidental brush of the skin would fluster me. I'd ordered a drink to calm my nerves, but it only made my reaction to him worse.

Now I'm standing in front of the mirror, wondering if I've chosen the right dress for the evening. It seems fitting since I've made the decision to talk to him tonight. I've been doing a lot of thinking since our last conversation, and believe I owe it to him to hear the rest of it. He made a lot of sacrifices, and I'm starting to realize I'm not the only one who's hurting. Every now and then I see the pain in his eyes. Maybe after dinner we can find a place to be alone and clear the air between us. I think it'll be a relief for both of us.

The last time I'd worn this, it'd been wrapped in a box with a pretty red bow on top. It's the nicest dress I own. I feel a sense of feminine power, and I will need all the strength I can get, if I go through the plans I have for the night. I press my fingers to my toenails, making sure the polish is dry enough, then step into my matching red stilettos, before shoving a pair of sandals into my purse. There's no way I can handle these three-inch stems for more than a couple of hours, but they're meant to go with the dress, and I like the way they accentuate my legs.

Leaving my hair down in loose waves, I make my eyes smoky the way Gia had shown me, then dust my lips in a nude gloss. I barely recognize my own reflection, but I'm satisfied with my appearance. Peeking at the clock, I try Gia on her cell phone, getting her voicemail. A few more minutes and we'll be late. I grab my purse and head next door, anxious to see what she's wearing.

"Hey, you in there?" I knock and wait for a response. "*Hello?*" I knock again. Pressing my ear to the door, there's not a peep on the other side. I assume they left already. It would've been nice for Gia to tell me.

I look for the restaurant on the casino map and make my way toward the elevators. Finally finding the sushi bar on the third floor, a beautiful brunette with shiny straight hair greets me with a friendly smile. Her name is Amy.

"Yes, I'm part of a reservation for six o'clock. It should be under Gia."

She opens a black book. A crease forms between her brows as she looks it over. "Could it possibly be under another name? I don't see a Gia."

They better not have cancelled without telling me. I swear I'll wring her neck. "How about Logan?"

Her eyes scan the book. "No. I don't have a Logan either."

"Do you have a Luke?" I don't know why Gia would put it under his name, but it's worth a try.

"Yep! I have a Luke." She smiles. "Follow me."

A surge of unwanted jealousy shoots through me. *I bet you do.* Squashing the thought, I trail behind her. The dimly lit restaurant's sophisticated, yet casual, style makes me feel at ease. When we stop in front of a small table, she pulls out a chair, then mentions something about our server, but I'm too entranced by the sight of Luke to make out her sentence.

Standing, he towers in a white button-up shirt that fits nicely over his broad chest and shoulders. His sleeves are rolled up to his elbows, showing off his muscular forearms. A loose tie hangs around his neck, and black slacks frame his long, lean legs. When I finally meet his handsome face, his penetrating gaze nearly knocks the wind out of me. And here I thought *I* was powerful … Ha!

I take my seat, watching his throat bob.

"You look…" The heat in his stare says enough. "Beautiful."

"Thank you." I clear my throat. "So do you ... not beautiful ... but handsome." My cheeks flood with heat. "Where is everybody?" I ask when he sits across from me, resting his forearms on the table.

"They ... uh ... passed out after we got back. Said to go without them."

I frown. "I'm right next door, and nobody thought to tell me."

"Is this going to be a problem?"

"What?"

"You and I alone together. We don't have to do this." A flash of hurt shows on his face, but the next moment it's gone.

"Listen, I'm sorry about the way I handled things. I ... I've thought it through and ... I'm ready to listen ... to all of it." I lick my lips. "I won't run away this time. That was immature of me. Once I was able to clear my head, it helped me see things differently. I know you would never intentionally hurt me. That just isn't you."

His body relaxes, and he leans back in his chair, studying me. His mouth tips up at the corners. "Really?"

I nod.

Continuing to look me over, he says, "Thought you'd never talk to me again, then seeing you in that dress." He shakes his head. "I'm surprised to see you wearing it."

"Why?"

"C'mon. You know why. Figured you'd burn it." He twirls the ice in his glass.

"I love this dress," I tell him, thinking back on the night I'd opened it. He'd come back for me, and I had betrayed him, falling into the arms of another man. The memory of the pain in his expression from the words I'd then spoken brings me close to tears. I hide behind a menu, not wanting to explain them.

We're saved from the uncomfortable silence when a waitress comes by to take our orders. Never being a fan of seafood, I go with a chicken dish, while Luke orders the sushi. Moments later our server brings by two bottles of Kirin Light and a small container of sake, along with two shot glasses.

Luke pours the sake into a shot glass. "Ever try a sake bomb?" he asks, cocking a brow at me.

"No. Never."

Pouring a third of his beer into a larger glass, he asks, "Wanna try one?"

"Okay," I say, grinning, my curiosity piqued.

Smirking devilishly, he repeats his earlier action, pushing the drinks in front of me. When our fingers brush, there's a surge of electricity.

Am I'm the only one who feels it, or does he feel it too?

"You okay?" he asks.

"Yeah, I'm fine." *Maybe he doesn't feel it.*

Picking up his own shot glass, he says, "This is how it's done." Dropping the entire shot into the beer glass, he swoops it up, and gulps it all down in one sip.

I squirm in my chair. "I'm not sure if I can do that."

"It's not as bad as it looks." He chuckles softly. "The beer mutes the taste of the sake when mixed together. I'm not gonna pressure you to do it, though, if you're scared."

"I'm not scared." I squint at him. Dropping the shot into my beer glass, I gulp down all the liquid, then slam the glass on the table, feeling very unladylike. "See?" I wipe my mouth. "Not scared."

He flashes his dimples. "Wow, you're a natural!"

My throat burns, but I play it off like I'm fine. "Learned from the best!"

"You want another?"

"Uh yeah, give me a minute."

"Gotta say, I'm impressed."

"Thank you." I sip on my water. We're both quiet for a moment, before he leans in, talking just above a whisper.

"So about this talk … when do you think we should have it?"

"The sooner the better."

"Tonight?"

I nod. "Not here, though. We could walk down the strip, find a place to sit maybe."

Leaning back, he takes a long pull from his bottle. "You sure you're ready?"

"I need the closure. Something tells me you need it too."

"All right then. It's settled. We'll do it tonight."

☆☆☆

By the end of dinner, we've cleaned every bit of food off our plates, and shared the rest of the sake. Our conversation is light, and we've had a few laughs, though most of them are at my expense. Luke talked me into trying a bite of his sushi. As soon as the gooey texture landed on the tip of my tongue, I knew I was in trouble. Closing my eyes, I tried to chew it fast then attempted to swallow, but my stomach protested. I involuntarily gagged, and Luke nearly choked on his food when he laughed.

After leaving the restaurant, Luke and I stopped by my room to drop off my heels. I was uncomfortably stuffed and didn't feel like carrying them. We took a slow walk down the strip, stopping at an empty bench in front of the Bellagio. And here we sit. The lights reflecting off the water has a calming effect, and we watch the fountains shoot toward the sky.

Luke lets out a long breath, looking out over the water. "He was a good man, Reese. Spent a lot of time with him."

I move closer, so I can hear him better. "My father?"

He nods once. "May not have seemed that way when you were a kid. Shit, I hated him back then. Seeing him hit you ... I wanted to hurt him." He swallows. "'Course I was just a punk kid then. The man I got to know years later wasn't the same man. He adored you." He finally looks at me.

"He really did change, didn't he?" My voice shakes with emotion.

"He hated himself for what he did to you, blamed himself for what had happened to you while he was in prison."

Warm tears roll down my face. What happened with Ronald was never my father's fault. "I'm glad you were able to see the good side of him." I sniff. "It just hurts because I miss him, you know? We had started to get close. Do you think ... do you think that when he died, he went in peace?"

He searches my face apprehensively.

"I don't mean physically," I clarify. "I saw the bruises, but ... he made amends with the people he'd hurt ... and he died doing what he loved."

Luke's eyes water, and he looks away. "Yeah. I think he went in peace." His response helps me relax a little.

"What did you talk about, besides what you were there for?"

Rubbing the stubble on his chin, he says, "Most of the time it was him doing the talking." He gives me a sideways glance. "He uh ... liked to lecture me a bit."

I frown, confused by what he means.

"It wasn't a *bad* thing. Just got deep, whatever the topic—God, forgiveness, alcoholism, church." He turns to me. "But mostly ... we talked about *you*."

I can't hide my smile. "You did?"

"All the time. He made me promise something."

"What was it?"

"He made me promise that if anything were to happen to him, I'd protect you." Looking me dead in the eye with the face of determination, he says, "No matter what happens, I'm keeping that promise. I owe it to him."

I have to look away from him. "Wow." I lick my lips. "That makes me feel like a burden."

"You know that's not true. Think about it."

I don't know what to think. My mind goes back to my dad. "Yesterday, at the hotel, what did you mean when you said my father wasn't supposed to be there?"

He drops his head. "Years back, Andrew and Glenn had a run-in. He'd arrested my father on assault charges. It would've been too risky for Andrew to go undercover. Glenn could've recognized him. So instead, he acted as a middle-man — sending messages from me to the Feds and vise-versa. It worked fine at first."

"Then what happened?"

"A man who partnered with Glenn put out a hit on me. Andrew tried to get me out, but the Feds weren't ready. They were too close to cracking the case, and they didn't want to screw everything up." His jaw clenches. "Then one day Andrew just showed up, said if they wouldn't help me, he would." Shaking his head, he continues, "Scared the shit out of me, seeing him there. I knew it was a bad idea, but the man was stubborn. He wouldn't listen."

I reach for his shoulder. "He is — *was* — stubborn. At the hospital, they told me there was only one other survivor, which I assume was you."

He nods.

"Then the man who shot him is dead, right?"

"Yes."

Blowing out a sigh of relief, I ask, "Did you know him?"

Anger simmers in his eyes. "Yeah, I knew him. Knew him well."

My pulse races. This is what I've been waiting for ... a name — *something*. The Feds had refused to disclose that information, saying it was for my safety. "Who was it? What was his name?"

His head falls in his hands, and he tugs on his hair, his fingers turning white. "I'm sorry. I tried to stop him, but it was too late." His words come out choked.

Seeing how much this is weighing on him is breaking my heart. Rubbing his back, I pull him tightly against my shoulder. "I don't blame you. You did what you could," I say softly, realizing he's crying.

"It was Glenn. My father killed him."

Chapter

LUKE

Eighteen

That'd been one of the hardest things I'd had to do in all of my fucked up life. It took a lot of fight not to break down in front of her. Not knowing what she was thinking nearly killed me. I couldn't look her in the eye until her words had forced me to, expecting her expression to be filled with hate—or worse, fear. I've got her father's killer's blood pumping inside my veins, and that's got to be hard for her. She should've been repulsed by the sight of me, but instead her gaze was sympathetic—almost understanding.

We'd talked a little longer, and I'd kept my answers vague, purposely leaving out some of the details that I thought could hurt her. She didn't need to know that it was *her* life Glenn had threatened. I didn't want to scare her, and I definitely didn't want her feeling responsible for any part of Andrew's death. Knowing her, she'd blame herself when she'd been innocent in all of it. Bringing up the fact that I'd also been shot, she'd asked about my injuries, saying she wouldn't have been able to handle losing the both of us. I'd kept my reply to myself. It seemed she handled things just fine without me before, moving on pretty quickly. Anger stirred inside me at the thought. I inhaled a breath, curling my fingers to calm myself down. *That douche is going to wish he'd never laid eyes on her by the time I'm finished with him.*

We sit and stare at the water for a bit, growing tired, before we decide to make our way back to the hotel in comfortable silence. I'd noticed her phone blowing up a couple times, but always just ignored it. I figured she was being polite. As we're stepping off the elevator, it rings again, and I look over. "You don't have to avoid whoever that is on *my* account."

Her face pales. "Oh, uh … No biggie. Probably just Gia apologizing." She fidgets. Her body language tells me she's lying, but I don't know why.

"So she's awake then," I reply, going along with it. We approach their door. "Wanna come in and talk to her?"

"That's okay." She averts her eyes. "It's late. I'll talk to her in the morning." My gaze slides toward her phone, then back to her guilty face, and she smiles at me. "Thank you again … for everything. I really regret that we hadn't done it sooner, but I take the full blame. I know you tried on many occasions."

Logan's voice rings out from inside their room, and she and I look at

each other.

"What the hell was that?"

She covers her mouth, and her face turns red. "My guess … they're gettin' dirty."

I raise my brows, then press my ear to the door, immediately regretting it.

"*Ah, yeah baby, you like that?*" he moans. A moment later I hear the sound of body parts slapping. "*Take all of it, baby. Ah yeahhh.*"

Scanning Reese's giggling face, I ask, "This is what you have to live with?"

She nods.

"Does he always talk like this?"

"More often than not," she says, grinning. "Wanna take my couch?"

"Absolutely!" I'm surprised she offers, and there's no way I'd decline.

Unlocking her door, she waves me in. "I can't promise it'll be quieter, but at least it'll be less awkward." When she moves to the closet, I stride toward the TV and turn up the volume, muting the noises from next door. She brings a blanket and pillow to the couch, and I give her gorgeous body a slow once-over. If I could, I'd stare at her all night. I have been staring at her all night, but it still isn't enough. My fingers ache to touch her. I do what I can to keep them at my sides.

She sees the way I'm looking at her, and a blush spreads over her cheeks. "I um … I'm going to take a shower. You're welcome to use it after me, if you want."

After unbuttoning my shirt, I toss it to the floor. "Thanks. I'll do that." Turning around, I set up my bed, unable to get the picture of Reese—naked, soapy, and wet—out of my head. My jaw clenches, and I blow out a slow breath, squeezing my eyes shut. A noise interrupts my fantasy. Glancing over my shoulder, I find her standing in the same spot, watching me with her lips parted. Desire floods her eyes, which does nothing for my already raging hard-on. "Thought you were gonna take a shower." If she wants me to touch her, she'll have to ask.

"Right," she says, clearing her throat. "I-I was going to tell you something, but got distracted." She blinks. "I completely forgot what it was." She looks at me the way I'd been looking at her earlier—with a sense of longing.

"Must not have been that important."

"I guess not."

When her phone rings beside me, I press the green button and toss it over to her.

She glances at the phone then back up at me. "Crap! Why did you do that?" she whisper-yells.

I cock a brow, confused. "Do what?"

"Answer my phone?"

"I don't know ... to be courteous." I shrug, "What's the big deal?"

Her eyes drop to the floor, then a second later it hits me. *The lie in the elevator.* "You're still talking to that asshole. Aren't you?" I ask,

unable to keep the growl out of my voice.

She backs away, covering the phone. "Quiet! He'll hear you."

"Like I give a shit!" My gaze bores into hers.

"I don't want him to know you're in the room with me!" she hisses, moving toward the bedroom, lifting the phone to her ear. The only words I'm able to make out are, *"Not a good time. No. I'm alone,"* and, *"That was the TV."*

I stand next to the bed, seething. *What the hell's going on with her?* If things are over with him, like she'd said, why does it matter, whether or not she is alone? Kicking off my pants, I sit on the edge of the bed in my boxer briefs, cracking my neck from side to side. I'd recognized that look in her eyes earlier. There was no mistake. She'd wanted me. *Hell maybe she wants him too.* Fuck that! I won't share her. And I sure as hell ain't touching her until she figures this shit out.

A moment later I hear the water running, then rest my elbows on my knees, my gaze aimed at the floor. She must have cut their conversation short. I'd be lying if I said a large part of me didn't want to step in that shower and claim her as my own, show her who she belongs to. I'm afraid I'd hurt her though. I'm too fired up, and I'd be far from gentle.

"Luke."

Lifting my head, she stands in front of me, still wearing her dress, chewing on her lip, clearly nervous. She should be.

"I know you're angry. I'm sorry," she says softly, her hair piled on top of her head. It shows off her graceful neck. I want to taste the skin there, run my tongue up the side of it, but this isn't about what *I want*. "Can you *please* help me with this?" Biting her lip, she turns around. "My zipper is stuck, and I can't get it down." When I stand up, she fidgets, stiffening her shoulders.

"Sure, gorgeous. I'd *love* to help you take off the dress."

I hear her gulp.

My fingers touch the spot between her shoulder blades. Leaning over, I run my nose along the side of her neck, breathing in her sweet vanilla scent. Goose bumps raise on her skin, and she shutters.

"It's not what you think, you know," she says breathily. She tilts her head, giving me more access. "I can explain."

Using my finger and thumb, I tug on her zipper, bringing it down to the small of her back. Her dress slides off her shoulders, falling to her feet. Without moving away from me, she teases me in nothing but a sexy red bra and matching lace panties.

Placing my hands on her hips, I pull her back against my front, grinding my arousal against her perfect round ass. I let out a groan, and she whimpers, arching her back. I press my lips to her ear. "Explain why you lied to me."

"I ... I was worried it would upset you."

Increasing my grip on her hips, I say, "You told him you were alone. Why?"

Her breaths come shorter, and she presses against me, but doesn't answer.

Hooking my thumbs into the sides of her panties, I ask, "Why'd you lie to him?" It takes all my strength not to touch her where I know she needs it most. I want to leave her body aching.

"I ... I don't know, but I swear it's over between us."

Not good enough. "Stop playing games." Grinding into her again, I drag my teeth across my bottom lip. "Mmm. You feel so good." It comes out as a growl.

"Luke." She tries turning around, but I don't let her. It'd be too tempting to kiss that pouty mouth. "I ... I'm not playing games."

"You know where I stand, what I want. Don't make me break my promise."

A frustrated noise comes out of her. "You're driving me crazy!"

"Likewise," I retort, licking the shell of her ear. "Tell me what you want."

"I want ... I want you to..." she hesitates, "I ... I want..."

Releasing her, I back away, though it takes every ounce of my strength. My nostrils flare. "You don't know what you want." She spins around to argue, and I point her toward the bathroom. "Get in the shower." I climb under the blanket, resting my head against the pillow, with my hands clasped behind my neck.

Reese narrows her gaze on the center of the blanket, where my hard-on makes a tent. "Why are you being so difficult?"

"Figure out what you want, then we'll talk about it." My eyes take their fill of her once again. She's testing my patience. "You're playing a dangerous game, Reese. Get. In. The. Shower." *Before I bend you over and bury myself inside you.*

She lifts her chin in defiance. "I don't like the way you're talking to me!"

"Fine. Get in the shower, *please*, then go to bed." I close my eyes. "See you in the morning, sunshine." She grumbles something to herself, then I hear her storm away.

☆ ☆ ☆

It's early in the morning, and I'm hard enough to break rocks, glancing at my surroundings, cursing when I find Reese's purse on top of the coffee table. I rub my hand over my face. *Damn, I thought it'd all been a dream.* The memory of her tight little body wiggling against me, the smell of her skin, and the sounds of her whimpering, brings a low rumble to my chest. It'd have been so easy to take her, right then and there, but I couldn't. The universe is set on keeping us apart—always has been.

Watching that dildo put his hands on her these last few months has been torture. I won't put myself through that again. Hell no. I'll move out of the condo—make sure there's some real distance between us—before that happens.

I grab my clothes and shoot Logan a text.

Ready 2 drink, buddy?

Already started. U next door?

Yeah.

Tell me u finally hit that last night.

I snort. Do me a favor. Don't ask.

Yikes. R U coming to the pool?

B there soon.

After I'm halfway dressed, I take a peek in Reese's bedroom, noticing she left the door cracked. She's asleep on her back, wearing a pair of cotton shorts and a thin tank top. Her dark hair is sprawled out over her pillow, and her pink lips are parted. I smirk at the sound of her faint snores. She's adorable; so adorable that I decide to order her breakfast, as part of a peace offering, feeling guilty for the way I treated her last night.

I'd been a total dick, punishing her for her feelings. I swear the woman brings out the caveman side of me. I'll spend the rest of my life doing what I can to make her happy. The thought that she might not want the same thing feels like a blow to the chest. Massaging the ache there, I slowly move toward her bed, then gently brush my lips against her forehead. This woman has no idea what kind of power she has over me.

Chapter
REESE
Nineteen

Bagels, coffee, and orange juice—that's what was waiting for me when I'd woken up this morning. Surprisingly, I'd managed to sleep until ten. Other than the breakfast, there'd been no sign that Luke had been in my room last night. He's probably still angry with me, assuming I have feelings for Sean.

I'd tried to tell him, but the words just wouldn't come out right. Seriously, what had he expected? I couldn't think straight with the way he'd been touching me. With the hard ridges of his body pressed against me, and his hot breath blowing down my neck, he had me at his mercy. *Good Lord,* it had been so long since I'd felt that kind of electricity. And if I'm not mistaken, he'd been just as turned on. The only difference? The man has the will power of a saint. I have no idea how he does it.

I find Gia lying on her back in her light green bikini, with her hair in two curly ponytails. She'd texted me earlier, saying they'd be at the pool when I got up. "Thanks for saving a chair," I tell her, spreading out two towels before lying down beside her.

"You're welcome, sleepy-head." She points to the small

table between us. "Got you a Pina Colada—whipped cream, no cherry."

"Ahh, thank you." It looks refreshing, and I take a drink. "Mmm, that's good. It seems hotter today."

"Yeah, sweating already and it's not even noon."

"How long have you guys been out here?" I squeeze some lotion onto my legs then rub it all in.

"About an hour, give or take. Figured you probably needed the sleep, which is why I texted instead of showing up at your door this morning."

"How very thoughtful of you."

"I'm a thoughtful person."

I shift in my chair uncomfortably, spotting Luke and Logan chatting in the water—sipping on beer. Luke looks gorgeous as usual. I start sucking down my drink, wincing when I get a brain freeze. "So what happened to you last night? Why'd you bail?"

"I didn't realize how exhausted I'd be from the combination of day drinking and hours spent in the sun. Hence the reason I'm drinking water." She tips her cup. "How'd it go anyway?" Leaning over, she adds, "And don't just say in went *fine*. I know he didn't sleep in our room last night. Better tell me everything." A sly look crosses her face. "Uh huh."

My gaze slides to the pool, then back to her. "Dinner was nice. And yes, he stayed in my room," I say quietly. "But nothing physical happened. Sorry to disappoint you."

She eyes me skeptically. "Why am I finding that hard to believe?"

"I swear it's the truth."

"Was there kissing? Cuddling at least?"

I shake my head.

"Then why'd he stay?"

"Are you kidding? There's no way I would've made him stay with you two! *You like that? Take all of it, baby. Ahhh yeahhh ohhhh yeahhh.*" I roll my eyes back for full effect, unable to hold back my grin.

Her big eyes widen. "Oh my God! You guys heard him?"

"We did."

She looks mortified. "What if other people heard?"

"I don't see how they couldn't. He's a screamer."

"I'm *so* embarrassed!"

"Why? It was all Logan. Besides, it's not like I haven't heard him before."

"I wonder if Luke's given him a hard time about it yet." She sprays herself with tanning oil. "So did you sleep in the same bed?"

"Nope. He took the couch and left before I woke up this morning."

She frowns. "Seriously?"

"Yep."

"Well that's *boring*. Tell me you two talked at least. You obviously had plenty of opportunity." She arches a brow, hopeful.

I feel Luke's eyes on me, then glance in his direction. Turning on my stomach, so he can't read my lips, I say, "There's so much I have to tell you, Gia. Yes, we talked. That's all I can say here." Tipping my head toward the pool, I add, "I'll tell you about it when we're alone."

She flips onto her belly. "Now, you got me *really* curious. He's staring by the way."

"I know."

We lie on our stomachs for probably twenty minutes, feeling

the heat. She wipes the sweat from her brow. "It's hot, and I'm getting hungry. Wanna get out of here? Go grab some lunch?" She wiggles her brows. "I'm ready to hear about this talk."

I'm about to agree, but I'm scooped out of my chair, letting out a scream when I'm crushed into a muscular chest. Luke carries me, smirking down at me, as if he were the devil. "What are you doing? Put me down!"

He strides toward the pool, soaking me with his wet, slippery body. My arms are flailing. The tips of his hair drip cold water down my neck. It feels good, but that's beside the point. "I don't want to go in … put me down or I'll hurt you!" I squeal, continuing to fight him, but it's no use. We're airborne, and a second later we're in the water, making a big splash. My laughter has me choking as we come up from under the water. "You!" I cough twice, smacking at his torso. "Are—" *Cough.* "A dead man!" *Cough, cough.*

His grin is so wide his dimples are showing. "C'mon. You *love* when I get you all wet." He winks, confident. "At least it seemed that way last night." I fight the urge to smack and kiss him at the same time. He gets a thrill out of teasing me. Well, two can play that game.

Wringing out my hair, I move toward him, watching droplets of water drip from his long, thick lashes, down his face, and onto his lips. His golden eyes blaze down on me with a spark of curiosity in their depths. I stand on the tips of my toes, lightly brushing my breasts against his chest on the way up. My nipples harden from the contact.

"You're gonna pay for that," I tell him. My voice is husky.

His eyes are instantly hooded. He angles his head closer, but doesn't dare close the space between us. I lift my chin, so our mouths are just a breath away from each other. He smirks, reading my face, knowing I'm playing his game. His tongue darts out to lick his lips, but neither of us move an inch, and he says, "Looking forward to it."

Chapter
REESE
Twenty

Trying on her fifth pair of sunglasses, Gia turns to me. "What do you think?" She poses the same way she'd done with all the others. They're black with large, square lenses. The sides have a studded, quilted pattern, and the shape is flattering on her face.

"So far, those are my favorite."

"I think so too." She checks out her profile. "Should I get them or keep looking?" Her stomach growls so loudly her eyes slide toward the young salesman—probably checking to see if he'd heard, which, based on his smirk, he most definitely did. "You know what, I'll take these," she tells him, turning to me. "I'm starving. You ready to eat?"

Thank God! Although Luke had ordered me breakfast, I'd barely eaten. My stomach had been in knots, so I'd barely had an appetite. "At this point I could eat anything."

"You should've told me."

"I didn't realize it'd take you this long."

"Can you tell us where we might be able to find some good greasy food, preferably inside the mall?" she asks the salesman after she finishes paying for the new glasses.

He points us in the opposite direction from which we came. "There's a sports bar a few stores down from here. My friends and I eat there all the time. Plenty of greasy food for you to pick from."

"Perfect, thanks!"

As we make our way toward the restaurant, Gia inhales. "Do you smell that?" We give each other a look, then hurry to the hostess station, relieved when we're seated without having to wait.

We order our food, along with a couple Diet Cokes, both steering away from alcohol, needing a bit of a break.

"You think the boys are gambling?" I ask Gia.

"Definitely. Logan seemed pretty drunk when we left the pool. I hope he isn't stupid with his money."

"I've only seen Luke that way once."

"What, drunk?"

I nod.

"It's sort of comical. Those two."

I agree. "They're so different, yet so much alike."

Our waitress comes out with our Philly on two separate plates, setting them down in front of us. "Here you go. Can I get you anything else?"

We shake our heads, declining, wasting no time scarfing it down. Minutes later, when there's barely anything left, Gia pops a fry into her mouth, leaning back in her chair. "*So* ... now that we've got food off the brain, I want to hear about you and Luke."

I take a sip of my drink and blow out a long breath. *Geesh, where do I start?* "You have no idea. So much has changed in the last few days. I could go on and on."

"So, tell me already!"

"I was wrong about him. Wrong about everything."

She pushes her glass to the edge of the table, signaling our waitress for another refill. "Go on."

I run her through the details of all that Luke had confessed to me. She doesn't seem as surprised as I'd expected. There are parts where I talk about my father, and we both cry. Our server walks by and drops off a stack of napkins, probably noticing our tears.

"I need to say something, but when I do, please don't hate me. I feel terrible for this." She sniffs.

The look on her face makes me nervous. "What is it?"

Her lip trembles. "I knew about Luke. I wanted to tell you, but he begged me to give him time to do it on his own. I hated keeping it from you. I swear. There were so many times I almost told you."

I don't even know what to say. I'm … I'm just shocked. "How long have you known?"

"About a week." She blows her nose, then uses another napkin to dab her eyes again. *Judging by the remorse she's showing, you'd think she'd been hiding it for months.* "It was right before we met up at Heartlands that night. Logan and I had been fighting. He'd gone over to Luke's place to vent—telling him that you and I had this *crazy* idea, that he'd gone off and gotten married." She chokes out a laugh, and I can't help but laugh with her. Yeah … we were *way* off on that one. "Anyway, Luke wanted to talk to me and set the record straight. That's when he told me everything."

"That's why Logan invited him to dinner." I gasp at the realization. It all makes sense.

She nods sadly. "Will you ever be able to forgive me?"

"Of course … I mean, sure I'm a little mad that you kept it from me, but I'll forgive you," I say reassuringly. "I know how convincing Luke can be. Besides, you'd only known for a week. I think if he'd waited much longer, you wouldn't have been able to keep it in."

"I wouldn't have. And I feel terrible for judging him so harshly. He was only trying to protect you."

"Trying to protect all of us," I add, and she gives me a confused look.

"What do you mean all of us?"

Leaning forward, I tuck my hair behind my ear. "Luke said that Glenn had threatened the people he loved. That's why he'd gotten involved in this whole thing."

"No. That's not what I heard. I was told that it was *your* life that was being threatened. Not anybody else's. That's the reason he called your father." She puts her tongue in her cheek.

Could she be right? Was it all just for me? It would explain why my father was so eager to help. My eyes lift to hers. "He's still protecting me. Isn't he? He doesn't want me feeling responsible ... for what happened to my father."

"But you don't, right?" She looks worried. "You *know* it's not your fault, Reese."

"I know ... I just ... what else did he tell you? What did he say about the night it all ended — the night of the shootout? Maybe there's more he hasn't told me. I ... I need to know."

She fidgets in her chair. "Okay, um ... well, most importantly ... he'd said that Glenn is the one who shot Andrew, which you know already."

I nod, remembering how hard it was for him to tell me. I'd never blame him for the sins of his father. They're nothing alike — not even close. "What else?"

"Umm, he'd said he tried to save him, but was too late. The last thing he remembers is pulling the trigger, but then someone shot him and everything faded to black."

"Wait, pulled the trigger? Who pulled the trigger?"

"He didn't tell you?" Her eyes are sorrowful.

"He never said anything about pulling a trigger. *Who* pulled the trigger?"

"Luke did." She sniffs. "He killed his father, trying to save yours. Shot him in the head. He died instantly."

Hot tears roll down my face. I grab a napkin, wiping them away, but they keep on coming. Luke did this for me—*risked his life* for me. How could I have been so blind? And look how I've repaid him.

"Oh my God! I have to go to him." I dig through my purse, and finally toss my debit card on the table, staring Gia in the eyes. "How will he ever be able to forgive me? I've completely betrayed him—after everything!" I picture the look in his eyes last night when he thought I was still talking to Sean.

She shakes her head. "Part of this is my fault."

"How?"

"I should've trusted your instincts, instead of pushing you to be with Sean."

"I made that choice on my own Gia. *I* should've trusted my instincts. Luke's been nothing but good to me, since the day I met him. Saved me repeatedly! I have to find him."

"Take your card. I don't need it."

"I'll get it back from you at the hotel," I reply over my shoulder, getting the attention of the other customers.

"I love you! Go get him and good luck!"

Yeah, I'm gonna need it.

Chapter
REESE
Twenty-One

My sole mission is getting him alone, where I can talk to him and tell him how I feel. I don't care about my pride anymore. No man has ever done something so selfless because of his love for me. He could've left for Brazil and trained to fight. He could've stayed in Phoenix and taken his chances. Instead, he put his life on hold in order to protect me, just like he'd done when I was a little girl. I swallow the lump in my throat, then press my tongue to the roof of my mouth, keeping the tears at bay. How will he ever be able to forgive me? My relationship with Sean had been rubbed in his face, and the jealousy he'd shown last night was warranted. He has every right to be angry, after going through hell and back for me, only to come home and find me with someone else. I can't imagine what that has been like for him.

The elevator opens and people start to shuffle out. I do a double take, finding Luke and Logan filling the small space in the very back—both grinning lazily when they see me. My heart swells at the way Luke's face lights up.

"Stay there," I tell him directly.

Judging by their bloodshot, watery eyes they continued their drinking after the pool.

"Looks like you're wanted," Logan grumbles.

Luke's dimples make an appearance. "Just got your text," he says, looking like the most adorable, yet sexiest man I've ever seen. And to think, he *loves* me. Something comes over me in that moment. I lose all control and jump into his arms, slamming our mouths together. He kisses me back—warm and sweet—and a groan escapes him. He tastes like alcohol and mint and everything that I've missed. My hands are all over him, before a snicker behind me interrupts us.

Releasing his lips, I try to catch my breath, throwing a dirty look over my shoulder. "Get out of here, Logan!"

"Wait. Where the hell's my woman?"

"On her way. She's fine."

"Why aren't you two together?" He frowns.

It's a logical question, but if I had to explain, it'd probably take me all day. "Look, I really need to talk to Luke. Can you give us some privacy, please? She'll be here any minute. I promise."

"Looks like *talking* isn't the only thing you *need* from him," he snorts, glancing at Luke, who tips his head toward the lobby, gesturing for him to go. "All right, all right. I'm out!" He steps out of the elevator. "Only because I owe you one." He points to Luke.

Luke presses our floor number, and I give him some room as the door slides closed. He eyes me curiously, then rubs the back of his neck. "You drunk?"

"I stopped drinking hours ago."

He tilts his head. "You gonna tell me why you kissed me?"

"Gia told me everything."

His brows bunch together.

"I *know* why you left. I *know* what happened with your father—why you were shot. Why did you keep that from me?"

His eyes roam over my face, and it takes a few seconds for him to answer. "Because, I know you. You'd blame yourself."

"You can't protect me from everything! You could've been killed; I don't deserve you putting your life on the line for me. The way I've treated you ... since you've been back—the things you've had to see—I'm sorry!" I frame his face with my hands. "God, I'm so sorry," I whisper, desperate to take his pain away. Standing on my toes, I bring our faces closer together, and our noses slightly brush. I can feel him holding back. "Luke please, I need you." It comes out as a cry, then he finally claims my mouth.

I drape my arms around his neck, fisting his hair. He kisses me with passion, leaving no part of my mouth untouched. Picking me up, he wraps my legs around him, and his erection presses against my panties. We moan in unison, and I throw my head back. He traces his tongue along my jawline, down my neck. My fingers have a mind of their own, bringing his shirt up and over his head. I run my hands over the bulging muscles of his tattooed arms, shoulders, and chest, then he devours my mouth again, changing angles, while our tongues twirl together. I hear the elevator ding in the background, and the door slides open.

He stiffens, pulling away, and I slide down his body. He looks as if a bucket of cold water has been poured over him.

"I guess we've reached our floor," I say awkwardly. He nods without replying. Turning, I stride out of the elevator, down the hall, with him following me. I stop in front of my room, grabbing the key card, feeling his breath hot on my neck.

"I shouldn't be here," his voice is gravelly. "My head is messed up. I've had a lot to drink."

The door unlatches, and I glance over my shoulder, forgetting I'd taken off his shirt in the heat of passion. "Please, I want you to stay," I say to his bare chest. He follows me inside, shutting the door behind him, then tosses his shirt over a chair. I'm pretty sure he's angry.

"Do you know what it was like seeing that prick put his hands all over you? Watching him kiss you day after day?" His nostrils flare, and I feel sick to my stomach. "It ripped my fucking heart out!"

"I'd give anything to take it back! I can't stand that I've hurt you; you didn't deserve it."

He steps toward me, 'til I'm backed against the wall, with his palms flat on either side of me. "Why are you yelling at me?"

Lowering the volume of my voice, I say, "I'm *not* yelling at you ... I'm yelling at myself!" My lip quivers. "I should've trusted you!"

"You never answered my question."

"About what?"

"Did you love him?"

I shake my head. "I've only ever loved you."

"You tell him you love him?"

I take a long, slow blink. "Yes ... but I was confused," I say, struggling to keep my gaze above his neck. "It's why I couldn't take the next step with him," I continue. "He couldn't stand that I was still in love with you—that you were all I could see—that I wouldn't touch him the way that I've touched you!"

"Yeah, why didn't you? 'Cause you sure let him touch you."

"It only feels right when I'm with you!"

Bringing his face inches from mine, he asks, "And why do you think that is?" His gaze is fierce.

"Because you belong to me, and I belong to you!" I grab his

face, our mouths colliding, and then one of his hands is in my hair, the other is rubbing down my back, and squeezing my ass. "I've been yours since the very first day I met you." I reach for his waistband and unbutton his jeans, and his breathing increases. Our movement becomes frantic, and I slip my hand inside his boxer briefs, stroking him like he'd once shown me. Kissing him deep, I move my grip up and down his long, thick shaft.

He hangs his head to watch what I'm doing. "You don't play fair," he groans.

"Neither do you," I reply, zoning in on the sexy V that flexes, while he lightly thrusts in my hand. I can feel myself getting wetter at the sight. Teasing my lips, he swoops me up, carrying me toward the couch. My dress is off within seconds, and my bra comes next. I shiver at his gaze, as he stares at my naked breasts.

He senses my nervousness. "This okay?"

I nod, biting my lip, before his eyes return to my breasts. My skin tingles in anticipation. After taking me in, he greedily cups my breasts together, bringing my peaked nipple into his warm mouth. I moan, pulling him closer, and he swirls his tongue, lapping at my nipple. Using his finger and thumb, he stimulates the other one. A current jolts between my legs, and I cry out, arching toward the ceiling. He feasts on my breasts, as if he is starving—nibbling and licking—with his arousal pressing against my thigh.

My legs shake. "Luke, please!" I whimper, needing him inside me.

"Told you, you would beg." Meeting my eyes, he continues his assault on me.

I reach for his jeans. "You're torturing me!" I try to get them over his hips, but he doesn't budge. "Please, help me take these off." If he wants me to beg, I'll beg.

Groaning, he shoves them down his legs, and I kick them off his feet. Shifting with just our underwear between us, he holds himself above me. I take my time, exploring the ridges in his back, over his shoulders, down the front of him. His body trembles when I trace the lines of his stomach, then his teeth graze his bottom lip.

Angling his head, he takes my mouth with his. Our tongues tangle, then he rocks against me, squeezing my breast. We moan together, and he circles his hips, pressing his hardness exactly where I need him. I arch into him, increasing the friction, then claw at his back. He releases my lips and slides his nose down my cheek. "If I take you now, I'll hurt you." He pulls back to look at me. "And the fucked up thing about it is, part of me *wants* to." He swallows.

My heart is breaking all over again. *I put that hurt on his face.* "Do it. I want you to hurt me."

His head drops to the crook of my neck, and he presses his lips there.

"Don't ... don't say that." Gripping my panties, he rips them off in one quick movement, shocking me. "You're soaked," he growls. He brushes the hair off my face, before his fingers trickle along my flesh. I squirm beneath him. Seconds later, one long finger slips inside me, and he swallows my moans. I grip his smooth, hard length, pumping him in my hand. He hisses through his teeth, adding another finger, and I can't stop the noises coming from my mouth. My body rises, and I follow his movements, wanting him to teach me.

"Feels so good," he whispers, licking the shell of my ear. "Does this feel good?"

"It feels amazing," I breathe.

"Damn, I should've left your panties on." Lifting my hips, he thrusts against me. "Ahh, it'd be so easy to just—"

"It's okay," I pant. "I'm ready."

He curls his fingers, stroking me deep. "Want it to be special," he says, barely able to speak. Both of us are dripping with sweat. I bite his shoulder to keep from screaming. "I'm not gonna last," he chokes, flicking his tongue back and forth over my nipple.

"Luke, I'm-I'm gonna—" My toes curl, and my legs tremble.

"That's it, baby. Come on me." His voice cracks right before my body explodes. We arch into each other, shuttering as we both cry out, our hearts beating in sync. He draws out every ounce of pleasure, until I'm limp in his arms. When it's over, he pulls back, gazing deep into my eyes.

"I love you," I tell him, needing him to know I truly do. He holds me tighter, then I run my fingers through his tousled hair.

He kisses my forehead. "Love you too."

Consumed with an overwhelming sense of guilt, and sadness, I break down in front of him.

Chapter
REESE
Twenty-Two

Being with Luke in that way again had brought on a flood of emotions. I'd felt like a piece missing from my soul had been returned to me. And to think—we haven't even had sex yet. I can't imagine how explosive it's going to be when it finally does happen ... which better be soon.

After the tears came, Luke had carried me over to the bed then tucked me under the covers. He lied down behind me, softly stroking my shoulder, while I cried. It had brought me comfort, but I internally cursed myself for being so emotional. I didn't want him to worry. And I definitely didn't want him thinking I'd regretted what we had just done. Aside from him having too much to drink before then—*his words- not mine*—I'd thought it'd been beautiful ... perfect really.

He'd continued to lay with me, and when my crying finally stopped, I rolled over to face him. The worry lines between his brows were prominent, and I'd smoothed them over with the pad of my thumb. He laid in silence, stroking my hair while I'd explained the reason behind my tears. I could see the relief in his eyes when I'd confirmed what I was feeling. He claimed my mouth again, kissing me until I was breathless. When he pulled away, he smacked me on the butt, and told me to put on some panties. I was tempted to tease him, but the man had already been tortured enough, so I'd done what he'd asked, and threw on a tank top, before slipping back into bed with him.

We both had a lot of questions, and this time we didn't hold back. I'd asked about his time away, about his father. I needed to know that he was going to be okay. I couldn't imagine what it'd been like to be in his position, to have to face what he did. The subject of Sean came up, and Luke's body would tense, but we talked through it. If we wanted our relationship to work, we couldn't avoid the hard topics. Our lack of communication in the past had only hurt us. I didn't want anything hindering us from moving forward. We talked for hours then drifted off to sleep, only to be awoken when our phones were ringing simultaneously.

I'd felt the bed dip, then Luke got up to grab his phone out of the other room. My gaze drifted up and down his defined body, as he confidently strode back. I grinned at the sight of his messy hair. I loved knowing that I had done that to him.

Memories of us when we were younger flickered through my mind — the crush I'd had on him, knowing he only saw me as a little girl, never dreaming that when we were older he'd return my feelings.

Meeting my eyes, he sets his phone on the nightstand then brushes his knuckles along my cheek. "What are you thinkin' about?"

"Memories ... you and me."

He sits on the bed, patting his lap. So I climb over and straddle him, placing my hands on his shoulders. His eyes burn with heat. He grips my hips, and I ignore the urge to move, feeling him harden.

"Was that Logan?"

"They want to meet for dinner."

"Mmm." I press my lips to the spot below his ear, and his thumbs circle the skin under the hem of my tank top. I continue the path down his neck. He trails his fingers up my back.

"You love to torture me. Don't you?" he asks, his voice gravelly.

"I think you've done your fair share." I pull back. He looks at my mouth then kisses me. I gently move my hips, moaning as our tongues dance together.

"Not even close." He groans, scooting me off him, then climbs out of bed, heading for the shower.

I make a sound of frustration as I stare at his perfectly round ass. I'll never tire of looking at him. "How much time do we have?"

"Not enough time for what you're thinking," he chuckles, turning on the water. "And I ain't rushing it, sweetheart."

☆ ☆ ☆

A waitress stands at our table holding a tray of plastic wands, filled to the brim with a clear liquid. The four of us had a late dinner, then ended up renting a VIP booth at Marquee nightclub. We're right in front of the dance floor. Logan and Luke sit at the ends, with Gia and me in the middle. She's had a perma-grin on her face since the moment she'd seen Luke and me hand in hand.

"Who's ready for shots?" Logan yells over the music, rubbing his hands together.

Luke and I lock eyes. I assume he's probably worried I'll drink too much and make a fool of myself, but instead he winks, and I smile back.

"We'll take eight of 'em," Logan says, holding up eight fingers.

"Eight?" Gia's brows arch, as he hands them over. "My stomach's still off. I can't handle drinking two of them."

"I'll take your second one," he replies. "Here, pass these over."

Luke holds the liquid under his nose, looking at Logan. "Tequila?"

"Patron. You guys want a lime?" he asks, holding up a cup of them. All of us pick one out. "I'd like to make a toast," Logan shouts, his shot in the air. "To Diaz winning the fight, and to *me* winning the jackpot."

Gia snorts. "I hate to be the bearer of bad news, honey, but it's not gonna happen."

"I thought he won two thousand dollars already." I nudge her, and she arches a brow.

"He swears he's gonna win ten more."

"Eight more," he corrects. "Hence the eight shots I ordered."

"Should I be worried? What if he becomes a compulsive gambler or something?"

He lifts his chin. "Don't believe me? I'll bet on it. Who wants to bet me?"

Luke taps his knuckles on the table. "I'll bet you. Gotta think of somethin' good, though." His lips twitch. "Give me a minute." He squeezes my thigh, and I glance between Logan and Gia.

An idea comes to my mind. "I got it!" I say excitedly. I lean in so everybody can hear me. "If Logan doesn't win the money, you two have to elope. And it *has* to happen before we leave!"

Luke chuckles, and Logan ponders the idea with a smirk.

Gia's eyes turn to slits when her head snaps to me. "*Hello!* Do *I* have a say in this?"

"What? You two always talk about getting married! I don't see what the big deal is," I say, feigning innocence.

"One, you shouldn't be encouraging him to throw away his money. Two, he hasn't even proposed. Three, he isn't going to win, which pretty much guarantees that he and I will be getting married! Four, I'd rather not have my wedding in Vegas, of all places! And five, my parents would totally kill me!" She crosses her arms over her chest.

"What if they don't know? We don't have to tell them," Logan mutters.

"You expect me to keep something like that from my mom?"

He shrugs. "Tell them, or keep it a secret. I like it, babe. You could still get the wedding you've always wanted, and have twice the fun." Her expression changes, and she squints.

I can tell she's considering it. "*So,* are you in?"

She tilts her head. "You *do* realize he's not gonna win the money."

"No faith in me," he says, disappointed.

She's told me repeatedly that this is what she wants, so they might as well make it official. She's just waiting for Logan to put the ring on her finger. "I guess we'll have to see."

Gia glances back at Logan. Their eyes lock, and a moment later she grins. "I can't believe I'm gonna say this," she says, blowing out a breath. "All right, I'm in." We all cheer excitedly. Logan and Luke bump fists.

"Are you sure? A bet is a bet," I tell her.

"Yes, I'm sure."

I clap like a schoolgirl, then we clink our shots together, pouring the liquid down our throats. My eyes water, and I make a bitter face, putting the lime in my mouth. "Blah! That was gross." I suck on the tangy juices. "Hard liquor is not for me. Do I have to drink the other one?"

Gia coughs and gags. "Yes! You owe me one for that."

"I'd say we're pretty even." I give her a look. She knows she screwed up when she kept Luke's secret from me.

"Hey, if you don't mind the possibility of wearing my vomit, then fine, I'll drink the other."

"Eww. Good point."

"All right. All right. Help me come up with somethin ladies."

Gia and I look at Logan with a blank face.

"What happens if and *when* I win?"

"*Oh, that.*" Gia smiles, her eyes slide to mine. "Same rules, different couple. If Logan wins, *you two* get married."

Wait. What?

Logan's eyes light up and he cackles. "Ready for marriage, bro?"

"I'd marry her," Luke says without hesitation.

My wide eyes lift to his. "You don't really mean that."

"I don't?"

"You do?"

"Why the hell wouldn't I?" He frowns, scanning my face. "What's it gonna take to convince you how important you are to me?"

I gulp, feeling a flock of butterflies in my belly. I'm not sure how to answer that exactly. I know that he loves me, but to hear him say he'd marry me without hesitation is a little surprising. *Could I marry Luke? Absolutely, I could.* "I know, I'm just…" Meeting his penetrating gaze, I softly say, "I … I'd marry you too."

He cups a hand behind his ear. "You what?"

"I'd marry you too," I repeat, my face heating.

"Damn right you will," he growls against my lips, practically pulling me on his lap, as he kisses me.

Gia interrupts our love fest. "*So,* are you in?"

I grab a lime and bounce it off her chest. My smile matching hers, I say, "Yes! I'm in!"

"Are you sure? A bet is a bet," she says, her eyes shining.

"*Yes*. I'm sure."

Luke and Logan are fist bumping again, then everyone except Gia tips back their second shot. It goes down smoother than the first one—for me at least. It doesn't seem to bother the guys any.

Once the alcohol kicks in, Gia and I are out on the dance floor, swaying our hips. Sweat beads along our skin, but we're having fun and aren't ready to stop yet. I hold up my hair, keeping it from sticking to the back of my neck, then strong hands grip onto my hips before a warm body presses behind me. I lay the back of my head against his powerful chest, unable to hide my grin.

"What took you so long?"

"How'd you know it was me?" His breath tickles my skin.

I spin around and lock my arms around him. "I always know when it's you. It's a feeling I get."

"Yeah?" he asks, pressing me flush against his hips. "There's a feeling I get around you, too." His thick erection rests against my stomach. "I like watching you dance," He smirks devilishly. "You're sexy."

"You gonna throw me over your shoulder and carry me out of here ... for old time's sake?"

"Depends."

"On what?"

"How many douchebags I have to fight off of you." He moves his hands down to my ass. "Though, now that I'm thinking about it, I might just carry you out for the fun of it." He kisses me slowly. When the music switches to something more upbeat, our kisses grow hungrier, and we're lost in each other. It's as if the rest of the crowd has disappeared. I can't stop touching him, kissing his addictive mouth.

"Dude, the kinky club is a mile down the street! Tone it down a little."

I look over in a daze, finding Logan and Gia dancing beside us.

She playfully smacks his chest, looking back and forth between us. "Do you two want to bow out early? We probably aren't gonna stay much longer."

Bow out early? I'm not ready to leave. I've only been to a club a couple times in my life. Plus, this is the first time Luke and I have been able to truly enjoy each other with nothing between us. It's hard to describe the feeling, other than the fact that it's relieving.

My eyes lift to Luke's, wondering if he's thinking the same thing—though he's probably tired of the club scene. I imagine he's done this several times with other women. I silently tell my mind not to go there.

"Havin' fun?" He cocks a brow at me.

I bite my lower lip, nodding.

"Good." He turns to them. "You guys go ahead. We're gonna stay." Leaning close to my ear, pressing a kiss there, he says, "I'll close out the bar if it makes you happy."

I pull back. "Are *you* having fun?" I ask, hoping this isn't just for me.

He makes a face. "Absolutely!" His dimples have me grinning. "Nowhere else I'd rather be."

Feeling an overwhelming sense of freedom, I let myself go. Our bodies stay in-tune with one another, both of us lighter. It's like telling whatever had been keeping us apart, that we're stronger, that we've finally won.

"You and me against the world, baby." He smirks. I stop moving and stare up at him.

He registers my look of shock. "What?"

"Nothing." I shake my head. "I was just thinking the same thing." If that surprised him, he didn't look it.

We danced all through the night, stopping only to get some drinks, or take a bathroom break. I hadn't realized how much my feet had been hurting until it was over. By the time we get back to our room, we are so spent that we pass out on top of the covers, still fully dressed and all.

Chapter
REESE
Twenty-Three

There's not one empty seat inside the arena at the MGM Grand Hotel. The crowd goes wild as they announce the main event. Gabriel Diaz, the Brazilian fighter, steps inside the cage, ready to defend his title. He stares into the face of his contender, and they bounce on their feet. A surge of adrenaline shoots through me. I get up on my tiptoes to see, when the guy in front of me blocks my view, raising his fists in the air. I attempt to peek around him, but it doesn't work. Luke squats down, tipping his head at me.

"Get on my shoulders."

"What?" I can barely hear him.

"My shoulders. Get on."

I look at my attire. "I can't. I'm wearing a dress!"

He smirks. "You're fine. My head will block anyone from seeing anything." He taps his shoulder. "Get on," he repeats. I do what he says, pulling down the back of my dress, covering my bottom, before he stands up. "Better?"

"Yeah!" I yell, able to see everything clearly, then Logan's squatting down, doing the same with Gia. We raise our fists, chanting like everybody else. The fight gets started, and the crowd quiets down a little, until Diaz lands a hard punch.

Beer splashes all over my legs, when the guy in front of me cheers. The guy looks back and apologizes.

"It's just a little beer," I say in Luke's ear.

He responds with a grunt as Diaz takes several more swings, landing most of them on the torso of his enemy. A loud roar erupts through the crowd, but the scenery changes when his contender gets him in a hold, taking Diaz to the floor. The bell dings, and seconds later the fighters go to their corners. Logan and Luke bend down, and we climb off their shoulders.

Strong hands cup my face, and Luke kisses me unexpectedly. He ends it with a soft peck to my forehead. He has one of those looks on his face, like he's having a moment. "It's all just sort of surreal, you being here with me."

"I know what you mean. Do you miss it?" His life would've been so different, if he would've kept fighting ... and kept me out of it.

He shrugs. "Not enough."

I don't know how to take his answer, but I let it go. The crowd gets louder as the fighters prepare for the second round, then Gia and I are back on their shoulders.

In the end, the judges call Diaz the winner, by unanimous decision. The men howl in agreement along with most of the crowd. I tap Luke on the head. When he looks up I bend down and plant a kiss on his sinful lips. I can't resist. He looks raw, and rugged, with a couple of days' old stubble on his chiseled jawline. His henley fits snugly over the ridges and dips of his muscles, and his tattoos are on display. My hormones are having a heyday.

After the fight, Logan suggests we all do a little gambling.

Gia and I stick with the quarter machines, while the boys look for something a little more high-risk. I'm up fifty bucks, and Gia's down twenty, give or take a few.

"I'd rather be shopping," she says monotone.

"I think most of the stores are closed by now." I click the BET ONE button when Gia's next statement freezes my hand midair.

"*So* there's a chance I could be pregnant."

What? My head snaps in her direction. "When was the last time you had your period? And way to bring it up."

She blows out a breath. "A couple of months ago, but my cycles have always been irregular. It's just ... I feel ... different. I don't know how to explain it."

"You're on the pill. Right?" I frown and she nods.

"I had to double up every now and then, when I'd forget to take them. I'm worried. I've been nauseous and emotional lately..."

She has been. "Have you said anything to Logan?"

"I want to take a test first." She chews on her lip. "That way, if it's negative, I don't have to say anything." Her eyes narrow. "If you tell Luke, I'll kill you. Keep this between us."

"I won't say anything. I promise." I make an X over my chest then check to see if anyone is around us. "Just so you know, if you *are* pregnant, Logan will be ecstatic—no question. He adores you." I picture their potential beautiful babies then cash out my quarters and get up. "I can't take it any longer. Let's go buy you a test. It'll give you peace of mind."

"I already bought one," she replies sheepishly. "I got it this morning."

My heart rate speeds up. "Did you take it?"

"No!" She cringes, standing up. "What if it's positive? Look at all the drinking I've been doing. I'm scared."

"You only drank heavily on that first day. If you're pregnant, I'm sure the baby will be fine ... but to be safe, I'd refrain from any more alcohol 'til you find out for sure. I'll tell the guys we're going to head back."

She grabs my arm. "I'd rather take the test at home. You know, in case it's positive." She makes a worried face.

"You sure you can wait 'til then?" I arch a brow at her. There's no way I'd have the patience, if the situation were reversed.

"It's just a couple of days." She shrugs. "I can wait."

I picture her toting a toddler around, with bouncing brown curls and big blue eyes that look just like hers, then another picture pops in my mind—a miniature Luke with tanned skin, a dimpled smile, and a pair of eyes that could melt you on the spot. Luke is going to make an incredible father.

"Why are you grinning like that?" she says, suspicious.

I'm getting way ahead of myself. "Just thinking."

"Uh huh. I know that look. You seriously need to get laid."

Speaking of laid, when we move out of the gambling area, I smile when I take a peek at my phone. Luke's ears must have been ringing. The moment I open the text, everything freezes, except for my thundering heartbeat.

"What's wrong?" she asks, shaking my shoulder. "Come on, Reese. You're worrying me."

I open my mouth, but am unable to speak. So I hold out my phone, and she takes it. A second later she's bursting out in laughter.

"You've got to be kidding me!" Her cell phone dings, then her eyes roam over the screen. "Logan just sent me the proof! *You two are getting married!*" She continues to giggle, reading over the amount of money that he won. "There it is." She shows me the picture of Logan holding up a check, then, wiping her eyes, her gaze falls over my shoulder. "Oh shit! Here comes the groom."

The look of love and determination radiating off Luke's face brings me a little out of my shock. The moment our eyes lock, he strides faster, then picks me up, swinging me around, pressing his lips to mine—hard and demanding. "Hey," he whispers with a crooked grin.

"Hey," I reply, breathless, sliding down his body.

"I'm gonna marry you."

When I fidget a little, he frowns, looking me over.

"We don't have to do this, if you're not ready." He runs his hands up and down my back in an effort to comfort me.

Of course I want to marry him. I've dreamt about it since I was a young girl. This is all just so sudden, and I'm still processing what we're about to do. I clear my throat, asking, "Are *you* ready?"

Glancing at Logan and Gia, he excuses us then moves us to a hallway near the restrooms, his hand on the small of my back. When he faces me, his forehead creases. "Look, I know what I want. I've known for a while now," he says, rubbing the back of his neck. "I don't care about the where's and whens, as long as you're with me," he says sincerely. "I know this isn't the most romantic situation. You've probably always wanted a big, elaborate wedding, but trust me, I'll do what I can to make it up to you."

My heart sinks. "I don't need a big wedding. That's not—"

"Let me finish." He pulls a small green box out of his pocket, dropping down on one knee. I cover my mouth with a shaky hand, disregarding the constant flushing of toilets. A short laugh comes out of him. "Sorry about that. For a moment, it was just you and me … not the best place for a proposal. I hadn't really planned this part out yet. Promise. I'm working on it."

I stifle a giggle. "It's okay. You can go on."

He exhales nervously. "You know, I bought this before we made the bet." Looking from the box back to me, he continues, "I knew I wanted to marry you. That part was easy. The hard part was figuring out when to ask you. Normally, I'm a patient man, but everything changes when it comes to you. All I could think about was putting it on your finger, letting everyone know that you're mine. I almost lost you once. I don't want to take that chance again. I can't." He draws in a deep breath. I get a glimpse of the boy I remember. "I never saw myself settling down. Never had the desire. Then you walked back into my life."

"*You* walked into *my* life," I correct with watery eyes.

"I walked into *your* life. You've made me feel things I never knew existed—taught me how to love, how to fight, how to be a better person. I know I don't deserve you…" He pauses and opens the small box. "But I'm asking you to take a chance on me, Reese. Marry me. Say yes."

I'm laughing and crying at the absurdity. Toilets are still flushing. The people passing through don't pay any attention. My strong, confident man now wears a mask of vulnerability, kneeling down in front of me. My beautiful guardian angel, my old friend, my long time crush. How could I not take a chance on him?

I can't keep the tears from leaking down my cheeks. "I'll marry you! Yes! I'll marry you!"

Relief washes over his features, as he slides the sparkly princess cut diamond on my finger. I cup his face, pulling him up, then he's towering over me with his signature sexy grin. I stand on my tiptoes, kissing each of his dimples, before finally meeting his lips.

Holy cow that's a big diamond!

Chapter
REESE
Twenty-Four

Gia and I got up early this morning with only a short time frame to find our dresses and get ready for the wedding. I had to find a dress that didn't need tailoring, and when I tried on the white, mermaid gown, with a plunging neckline, we both gasped at how well it fit to my body. "That's the one," Gia said immediately. I glanced over my shoulder and agreed. It wasn't as pricey as some of the others, which was also a big plus.

A couple hours later we found Gia's dress on display in the window of a bridal shop. The charcoal color had complemented her skin tone. The hemline hit right below the knees, and it was strapless, showing off her delicate collarbone. I loved it. We used the time it took to get some quick alterations done on Gia's dress to get our facials then later had our toenails and fingernails painted in a shimmery shade of pink. It took a load off knowing that Luke was handling his part of the arrangements, but at the same time I didn't know how he was going to do it. Most guys aren't really *into* this kind of stuff. I never expected a fancy wedding. I never expected I'd get married.

Luke had found a beautiful spot overlooking the lake. I think the owner had recognized him and pulled a few strings. He made the place available for a sunset ceremony. Now, with minutes left until the wedding, I'm a bundle of nerves. We didn't have time to get our hair done professionally, so I trusted Gia to do mine. I'm wearing it up, and she framed my face with a couple of ringlets.

"You look beautiful," Gia says, fanning herself.

"Thank you. So do you."

"Stop fidgeting. You're going to be fine."

I feel myself sweating. "Is there make up running down my face?"

She looks me over and shakes her head. "Luke's gonna drool when he sees you." She glances at the time. "I better get up there. You ready?"

"Yep," I say, shaking out my fingers.

She gives me a hug. "I love you."

"Love you too." I let out a breath as I watch her leave.

We'd chosen to write our own vows, and even though I'd memorized them, I don't trust myself not to get stage fright once I'm up there. So I'd written them down on a small piece of paper. Folding it in my hand, I walk out the same door Gia just exited.

My heart leaps in my chest as soon as I see him. My future husband stands waiting at the altar in a black tux. He's so incredibly handsome I almost lose my step as I move toward him. His perfect square jawline flexes, as his gaze slowly slides down my body then back up. I don't take my eyes off him, feeling that pull drawing me in. In my peripheral vision, Logan, Gia, and the preacher stand in their places. When I come to a stop inches from Luke, Gia snickers, and I look over.

I'd forgotten to hand her my Calla lilies. Our eyes meet, and she winks.

"Sorry." I blush, giving her my flowers, then turn around to face Luke. His eyes clearly speak what he's thinking—that he loves the dress.

"Hey," he says, feeling the folded up piece of paper when he takes my hands.

"Hey." I grin.

His thumbs glide over my skin. Again, he looks me over. A smirk reaches his lips. He turns to the preacher and asks, "Any chance you could speed this up?"

"I'll do what I can," he answers with a chuckle.

Luke's gaze is back on me. "Waited a *long* time to get this woman alone. Don't think I can restrain myself much longer."

Everyone laughs, and my heart rate increases. I'd been thinking the same thing. Glancing at the preacher, I blink a couple times, sensing I know him from somewhere.

He stretches out his hand. "Honored to be here. You look very lovely this evening."

My eyes go wide, and it clicks. "I remember you." I cover my mouth. "You spoke at my father's funeral. How? How did you know?" I turn from him to Luke, who just shrugs.

"He's the pastor of your father's old church. He mentioned him to me a few times."

"Pastor Brian," he says, officially introducing himself. "Andrew was a good man. I can see the likeness between the two of you."

I nod, teary-eyed. I do look exactly like my father. "Yes. Thank ... thank you for coming."

He gestures to Luke. "This handsome fellow here is the one who arranged everything. Andrew was right about him. It's clear he really loves you."

I look up at Luke. "I really love him too," I say, planting a kiss on his lips. "Thank you."

"Hey! Supposed to wait 'til the end to do that," Logan cackles.

"I don't know how you did it," I say softly.

His eyes sparkle. "Don't worry about it."

We move on with the ceremony. I nervously read my vows, and even with the paper I still manage to fumble over some of the words. Luke speaks his from memory, tugging on my heartstrings with everything he says. The whole experience seems unreal—like I am in some sort of dream.

By the time the preacher announces us husband and wife, Luke is framing my face and then we kiss. My body comes alive, and I am lost in him. When his hands roam down my back, stopping on my ass, Logan whistles, reminding us of where we are.

Luke growls against my lips with hooded eyes. "You wanna get out of here?"

I nod and we politely say our goodbyes, thanking Pastor Brian once again. As soon as we step outside, Luke picks me up, taking me to a limo parked against the curb. Barking orders to the driver, he sets me down, lightly pushing me into the backseat.

"Whoa," I laugh, never seeing him this anxious, but it excites me.

I straddle him the whole ride over. Our soft kisses start out slow, quickly heating, as soon as our tongues collide. We can't stop touching each other. He kisses me deeply, squeezing my hips, rocking me against his erection. My stomach growls, ruining the moment. I blush when he pulls back to look at me. "We need to get you fed," he says firmly. I want to protest, but know it won't do any good. Luke's priority is to take care of me—always has been. I think it's about time that I take care of him.

Chapter
REESE
Twenty-Five

When we arrived at the hotel, he carries me over the threshold into the upgraded suite he'd gotten us. He's continued to surprise me with his thoughtfulness, keeping a small distance behind me while I walk around and take in everything. In the kitchenette, I find a bottle of champagne and a large selection of chocolate-covered fruit. Candles flicker around the edge of a jetted tub filled with rose petals and bubbles. My insides warm at the thought of using it.

I've changed into a shorter white dress—more comfortable—and now we're standing out on the balcony, enjoying our fruit tray and sharing the bottle of champagne. I rest my arms on the ledge, looking out over the city. "Thank you for all that you did today. The arrangement you made with the pastor ... it really meant a lot to me."

He shrugs. "You agreed to marry me. It's the least I could do."

"I'm lucky to marry you," I murmur. "I bet if my father could see us right now, he'd think we were crazy—eloping in Vegas." Looking across the night sky, it's hard to see the stars with all the casinos lighting up the strip.

"I *am* crazy ... crazy for *you*."

"If you haven't yet noticed, you don't have to sweet talk me anymore. You already have me. But I'll admit, you're good with your words." I grin, and he grins back.

"I'm gonna show you just how good I am."

"Is that a threat or a promise?"

"Both."

I look away, feeling excited and bashful at the same time.

"You nervous?"

"No," I lie. It's silent for a moment, and I drain the rest of my glass.

"Still hungry?"

"No." I bite my lip. "Well, maybe, but ... a different kind of hungry." I don't look at him when I say this. He doesn't respond either. "I can feel you staring."

"Does it bother you?"

"The way you're looking at me right now ... yes and no."

"Care to elaborate?" There's humor in his voice.

"You look like you want to eat me." I blush. "It makes me feel desired. What woman doesn't want to feel desired?"

He moves toward me, gripping my waist, before pulling me against him. "So you like feeling desired?" He trails kisses down my neck, his breath hot on my skin.

"Yes."

He tugs on my earlobe. "Tell me what you don't like."

I shiver. "Um ... my brain gets all foggy, and sometimes it's hard to breathe." The words come out shaky.

"Like now?" His tongue glides up the side of my neck.

"Yes, like now."

"What about your heart?"

"My heart? It races."

"You don't like that?"

I stretch my neck, as he continues to kiss the skin there. "I like how I feel. I don't like losing control." I swallow. "When I'm with you, it's easy to lose control."

The balcony door slides open, and he moves us inside. His fingers pause on the zipper at the back of my dress. His eyes search me. "Do you trust me?"

"More than anybody."

Slowly unzipping my dress, he slides the material down my body and over my hips. When it falls to the floor, his eyes glaze over. "First day I saw you, back at the gym…" A short laugh comes out of him. "Threw me off balance seeing you all grown up. I knew I was in trouble," he says, lifting my chin. "So many ways I've thought about making you come. So many times I've fantasized about it."

My breath hitches. "You thought about it from the beginning?" He nods once. I hadn't known he'd felt that way back then. "If that's true, you're a great actor."

He takes the clips out of my hair, and it spills over my shoulders. "Didn't matter what I wanted." Searching my eyes, he adds, "I knew you deserved better than me."

I completely disagree. "Luke?"

"Hmm?"

"Now that I'm yours, will you show me what you've wanted to do to me?"

Framing my face, he crashes our mouths together. I tear at his shirt, gasping from the intensity. The buttons fly off, and scatter on the floor, as our tongues slide together. He angles his head, palming my breasts in his rough hands. I glide my fingers over his sculptured chest, down the planes of his stomach, and he shudders beneath my touch. I work to take off his jeans, my body burning with so much need it almost hurts me. Picking me up, he kisses me harder, cupping my ass. I wrap my legs around him then we're moving. When my back meets a cold, hard surface, I rise up on my elbows, sprawled out on the dining table. Luke sits in a chair between my legs.

I laugh nervously. "Wh … what are you doing?"

He trails wet kisses along the apex of my thighs. Spreading them open, he licks the center of my panties. A strangled moan escapes my lips, and his eyes darken. He focuses between my legs, sliding my panties right off me.

"The first time you come as my wife, I'm gonna taste it." The words alone have me soaked. Bringing his face to my center, he slides his wet tongue along my crease in one slow lick, then another, and another.

The back of my head thumps against the table. I cry out, grabbing a fist full of his hair. He strokes me with his tongue in the same way he kisses my mouth. It feels wonderful. It feels dirty. It feels absolutely amazing. Over and over he licks me, firmly gripping my hips, as I desperately try to move them. "Luke," I whimper.

"I always knew you would taste like this," his voice rumbles. "Don't wanna stop."

"I don't want you to stop. Please don't stop."

He grunts his reply, sliding a hand up my stomach to play with my nipple. The other hand pushes a finger inside me. I arch into him when he adds another. I'm close to coming. My quiet whimpers turn into desperate moans, as he skillfully hits all my erogenous zones. "That's it baby." He licks again. "Come for me."

When his mouth moves over my clit, he switches between sucking and lightly using his teeth. My vision blurs, and I soar, exploding all over him. In the background I hear him groaning, then I fall into a post-orgasmic haze.

I don't even realize I'm being carried until my eyes open, and he lays me down on the bed, crawling over me. His thumbs hook into his boxer briefs, pulling them all the way down. I reach over and grip his hardened length.

His eyes close when I stroke him. I bend down and try to put him in my mouth, and he stops me with a strangled laugh. "If your mouth goes anywhere near my dick, I'm not gonna last."

"I want you to teach me how to do it."

Kissing me softly, he says, "I'll teach you a lot of things. I look forward to it." He kisses my jaw, down my neck, to the tops of my breasts. Moments later, his tongue flicks over each nipple. I grip the back of his head, pulling him toward me. I'm ready for more. He slides up my body, stretching my wrists above my head. His nose runs along my cheek, then he presses his lips against my ear. "I need to feel you bare, Reese—skin to skin."

My heart rate picks up, and I swallow back my nerves, but I know Luke will be gentle with me, if I need him to be.

"You ready?"

"Yes," I nod slowly. He gazes deep into my eyes then his fingers move between my legs, eliciting a moan out of me. I arch into his hand, trembling at every touch. "Luke, I'm aching." *I need more ... more of him.*

"Shh ... I got you," he says. We stare at each other, then he reaches down to take his tip and rubs it along my entrance. The warmth has me lifting my hips. He eases in slowly. I instinctively grab his shoulders, tensing, my teeth clenched. It doesn't hurt, but I'm preparing for it.

His forehead bunches. "Need me to stop?"

No way do I want this to stop. "No. It doesn't hurt yet."

He kisses me. "I'm barely in."

"I know. Keep going."

He inches forward, and his jaw goes tight. "This part may hurt. Hold on to me, okay?"

"I trust you," I whisper.

Several emotions pass over his face, then he lifts my hips, and thrusts all the way in. I cling to him with a death grip, my nails digging deep into his skin. He freezes. "You okay?"

I force myself to relax, feeling him stretch me. "It was just a pinch." Stroking his hair, I kiss his soft, warm lips to reassure him.

He presses our foreheads together, giving me time to get used to him. "You feel incredible," he breathes.

"You can move. It doesn't seem to hurt anymore." *Not at the moment, at least.*

"You sure?" He strokes my cheek.

I nod, as he watches me intently.

"I love you," he whispers.

"I love you too." My fingers follow the dips of his back, then he pulls all the way out, and thrusts back in. Closing my eyes, I urge him to keep going. He continues to move at a slow, torturous pace. The groans he makes, and the look on his face, adds to my arousal. His sweat drips onto my skin, and I lift my hips, wanting more friction.

"Good?"

"Yes, so good." I notice him shaking. "You're trembling," I pant.

"You have no idea how good you feel." He kisses me. "Hard to hold back."

"I don't want you to hold back."

"What do you want?"

I moan when he circles his hips. "I want more."

He drives into me harder, dragging his teeth across his bottom lip. I want to bite that lip. He does it again. "Like this?"

"Yes!"

His eyes blaze, and he plunges into me, growling. I squeeze his muscular ass, and he picks up his pace. Our mouths crash together, then I'm meeting his every thrust, loving the feel of him inside me. "More, baby?"

"Yes! Please! Harder." I don't even recognize my own voice.

Sliding down my body, he picks up my legs, placing them over his shoulders. He runs his tongue from my pelvic bone, up to my neck, settling right where I need him. "You were made for me," he grunts, driving into me in one hard thrust. I cry out in pleasure, as he continues. Over and over, he moves exactly how I need him—every time a little rougher than the last. "Tell me you're mine."

I thrash underneath him. "I'm yours."

Pounding into me harder, brushing his open mouth against mine, he says, "Look into my eyes when you say it." He traces my lips with his tongue, rolling my nipple between his fingers.

My body shivers, and I force myself to meet his smoldering gaze. "I've always been yours, and you know it."

"That's right," he growls. "You've always been mine." Plunging in and out of me, he hits a spot that has me shuddering in ecstasy. I curl my toes, crying out. He watches me, with his movements slow and deep, then he drives out his own release. A low, animalistic sound comes out of him, as he pulses inside me. His head falls to the crook of my neck. Rolling off me, he pulls my back against his front, then his lips lightly feather over my shoulder. He holds me tighter, and I smile at his sigh of contentment. It's in this moment that I realize what it's like to be truly happy.

Chapter

REESE

Twenty-Six

Two Months Later

Luke and I had moved my stuff into his place right away. Marriage has been quite the adjustment, but in a *very good* way. Sometimes I have to convince myself that I'm not dreaming, that Luke and I are really together. Nothing feels better than waking up and feeling his strong arms around me, his warm breath over my skin. He makes me feel safe, loved, and happy.

"Is this really necessary?" Gia asks.

"Yes," the men say together.

We're riding, blindfolded, in the back seat of my new Rover, quite an upgrade from my old, broken down Honda, unaware of where the guys are taking us. We're both antsy, and they keep ignoring our questions, getting a kick out of making us squirm. Luke insisted on going car shopping shortly after we'd gotten back, saying that he liked the idea of me driving an SUV.

The engine jerks forward, and my hand lands on Gia's lap. "Careful with my pretty car, and don't forget, there's a pregnant lady back here."

"Yeah! You don't want me getting sick in here, do you?"

"Sorry girls," Luke grumbles.

"You all right?" Logan asks her.

"I'll be all right when I get this thing off my face. It's giving me motion sickness."

Luke apologizes again. "I'll drive more careful.

After her pregnancy test came back positive, Gia freaked out, and took several more, thinking the result would come out differently. By the time she'd seen the doctor, she was already twelve weeks along. I'm thrilled at the thought of becoming an aunt, and Logan is ecstatic about being a father, which didn't surprise anyone. They've been planning a wedding, and Gia's parents took the news better than expected.

"How much longer?"

"Almost there, baby," Luke replies. "Just another minute."

"I better be blown away," Gia murmurs. "This is seriously torture."

"Whattya think, Luke? They gonna like it?"

"Maybe, maybe not," he grumbles back. "Women are difficult creatures."

"Pshh. You don't have to tell me."

They chuckle, and I glare behind my blindfold, though I'm not really mad. Finally, the car slows before coming to a stop.

"All right!" Gia claps. "I'm taking this thing off!"

"Not yet," Logan calls back. "I'm comin' around to get you."

She makes a noise of frustration, and I giggle as our doors open, and then I feel Luke's calloused hand on mine. He helps me out of the car, and we take careful steps, his other hand on the small of my back.

"Be careful with her Logan."

"I got her."

Luke presses his lips against my ear. "Did you peek?"

"No, but if I fall, you're gonna get it."

He chuckles lowly. "Ready?"

I nod. "Yeah, ready."

He unties my blindfold, then my eyes adjust on a large, single-story home, resting on a couple of acres.

"Where are we?" I ask.

Tugging me behind him, he leads me toward the house.

"Let them go in alone," I hear Logan mutter, as I glance over my shoulder, meeting Gia's eyes. She just shrugs, looking perplexed.

Luke picks a key off my keychain, unlocking the door before nudging it open.

Why would he have a key? We step inside, and my mouth drops. This place is gorgeous, with an open concept floor plan, and extremely tall ceilings. The back wall is covered in windows that frame views of the mountains. I walk around, taking in everything. Down the hall, to the right, sits a large kitchen and giant island, perfect for entertaining. White cabinets complement the dark hardwood floors throughout the home. Luke follows me to the other side of the house, watching me carefully. We've toyed with the idea of moving. *Could this home be a possibility for us? Is that why he brought me here?*

Crime has picked up in our area, and there's still a predator on the loose. Three murders and two attempted kidnappings have gone unsolved, all happening within the last three months, and within a two-mile radius of our home. Police say that all the cases are linked. Every victim was a young female, between the ages of thirteen and twenty-five. They've had a lot of leads, but the suspect is still at large.

There was an incident the other night, when Luke had gone

out for groceries. Chance and I were lying on the couch, watching television. Out of the blue, his ears had tipped back, and his fur stood up. He was growling, focused on the sliding glass door leading to the back. At first I'd tried calming him, not thinking anything of it. I couldn't see what he was staring at, but my view had been distorted from the light in the living room. When he'd bared his teeth, standing on all fours, it'd started to concern me. I'd never seen him so riled up. I stood up and flipped off the light, then scanned the yard, giving up when I couldn't find anything. As soon as Luke got home, I'd told him about what had happened. He'd checked the perimeter, coming up with nothing out of the ordinary. He'd praised Chance, given him a treat, then mumbled something about how our neighborhood was going to shit.

"Tell me what you're thinking," Luke murmurs.

I turn to face him. "I'm thinking there's only one reason you'd be showing me this."

He watches the emotions play over my face. "What's the reason?"

Tears prick the backs of my eyes. "Is this ... is this ours?" I cover my mouth with a shaky hand.

He answers with a single nod.

"It must have cost you a fortune."

He brushes a kiss against my lips. "The general contractor was upside down on it—needed a quick sale. Came and checked it out. Liked what I saw. Figured it was plenty big enough to grow a family." Gripping my hips, he pulls me toward him. He presses our foreheads together, wiping a tear from under my eye with the back of his fingers. "I pictured you living in it, decorating it the way you like, making it yours." He shrugs. "I don't know. It just ... fit."

"What about you?"

"Me?"

I arch a brow at him. "Was I by myself when you had this mental picture?"

"Oh ... that." He grins. "I was there, too, wondering what the hell I'd done right to end up with someone like you." Squeezing my bottom, he pulls me in for another kiss, then tugs on my bottom lip.

"I don't even know what to say. Thank you isn't enough ... it's perfect." Then realization hits me. I'd almost forgotten. "Wait!"

His forehead bunches.

"Tell me Gia still gets a surprise too."

He relaxes. "Yeah. It's right next door."

"What?"

Letting go of me, he strides toward a window that faces the front. "Logan bought the other acre. They'll stay at his place while they build on it — move in a little after us."

"We're going to be neighbors again?"

He waves me over, pointing. I find Logan and Gia standing in the lot to the right of us. It couldn't get any better.

Jumping into his arms, I wrap my legs around him, kissing him all over. "Thank you! Thank you! Thank you!"

He chuckles. "Welcome, baby. Anything to see that smile on your face."

"Words can't describe how happy I am." I glance over my shoulder. "Do me a favor. Tell them we're gonna be a minute. Maybe they can leave and come back." He sets me down with a curious expression.

I back away from the windows, pulling my shirt up over my

head. His eyes turn into liquid as he stares at my chest. I head toward the master bedroom, unbuttoning my pants. "Hurry up already, would ya?"

His mouth tips up at the corners. "Yes, ma'am!"

Chapter
REESE
Twenty-Seven

We'd found out, shortly after Vegas, that Sean had moved out of the condo. I don't know if his moving had anything to do with me, but I wondered. Before we'd gotten home, I'd made Luke promise not to touch him — not that Sean doesn't deserve it. I wouldn't put it past him to sue Luke for all he is worth. In return, Luke requested I stay away from him. That wasn't hard to do, since he hadn't been around ... until now.

Luke and I had driven separately to work so he could workout after. Sean sees me pull up and leans against his car with his arms crossed, waiting for me. I try to act like I don't seen him, but I'm not that good of an actress. With my head down, I place my hand on the door handle, pushing the car door open.

Sean stands right in front of me. "Nice ride."

I get out of my car. "What do you want?"

"To talk."

"I thought you moved."

"Yeah I did," he says, glancing toward his old house. "Will and I are hangin' out tonight."

"Sounds fun. I'll let you get to it." I click the alarm and turn to walk away, but he grabs me.

"Wait. Will says you're living with him now. That true?"

I eye the spot where he's touching me. "Is that any of your business?" I arch a brow. "But yes, I am. Let go of my arm, please."

"Sorry." He releases me, but isn't finished. "Listen, I'm not a bad person. I *did* care about you, Reese. Still do," he says, serious. "I miss you."

Let him down gently. "You don't need to worry about me, and I don't think you're a bad person. To tell you the truth … you were right. It never would've worked between us. I've been in love with Luke since my childhood, and I wasn't being fair to you."

He doesn't look happy by my admission, kicking a small rock out of the pathway. "Guess we'd have been better off as friends, huh?"

"Guess we'll never know. What's done is done," I say bluntly. The words are harsh, but true. "I wish you the best. I really do." *In other words, get out of my hair.*

"I wish you the same." His eyes meet mine, and he holds out a hand. "Good luck to you, Reese."

"Good luck," I reply hesitantly, taking it. He pulls me into a hug. It's awkward, and I don't know how to react. At first my arms are at my sides, then I slowly pat him on the back, hearing the roar of a familiar Harley.

My pulse races, and I let go of him, but he holds me in place, squeezing me tighter, our chests pressed together. *Damn him!* "What are you doing?" I hiss, struggling to break free. "Let go of me!"

He rubs my back, his hands moving downward. "It's okay," he murmurs. "I'm here."

Um, what? I'm ready to knee him in the balls, when he's

suddenly ripped away from me.

"The fuck!" Luke stares him down, his gaze feral. "Get your hands off my wife!" His arm swings back, before his fist slams directly into Sean's jaw. Sean flies to the ground, and Luke towers over him, ready to swing again.

"Stop!" I scream. "We were saying goodbye. Nothing happened, I promise!"

Luke stops himself, glancing over. Anger and hurt fill his features. *God, he saw us hugging. Sean was taunting him.*

Sean gets up, staggering, his hand over his mouth. Blood seeps through his fingers. "Your wife?" he scoffs. "*You* married him?"

"Yes. I married him." I lift my chin.

He snorts, licking blood from the corner of his mouth. "Funny." He looks at Luke. "You failed to mention that earlier."

"Goodbye, Sean." *I wish he would just shut up. He's making things worse, obviously on purpose.*

With a look of disgust, he chuckles, "You know what? You two deserve each other."

Luke points. "Get off my property! You better fuckin' hope I don't see you again. I won't go as easy on you next time."

"I'm gone," Sean retorts, heading straight for his car. He starts the engine and speeds off, just as Luke turns his angry gaze on me.

I drop my eyes to the hand that he's flexing—the one he used to hit Sean. "Are … are you hurt?"

His jaw flexes, and he looks me over. "You hide it from him on purpose?"

My heart sinks. "No. It may have looked that way, but—"

"What was he doing here, Reese? You were hugging him.

You miss him or somethin'?"

"Of course not. You're making it more than it is. I pulled in the driveway, and he showed up. One second we were saying goodbye, the next he was hugging me."

"And in the process, you failed to mention that you were *mine*." He glares.

"He asked if we were living together, and I told him yes." Narrowing my eyes, I asked, "What exactly are you implying?" *I know what he's implying, and it enrages me.* "I went to work. I came home. It's not my fault he trapped me at my damn car!"

"Trapped?" he snorts. "Your hands were all over each other."

That sets me off, and I get in his face, seething. "Screw you if you don't believe me."

"Sorry, princess. I'm not in the mood."

I open my mouth, then angrily move past him, headed for Logan and Gia's.

"That's it. Run away like you always do," he grumbles.

When I spin around, he's waiting for my angry retort. Instead, I say something he isn't expecting. "I hurt you in the past, and I'm sorry. I'd give anything to take it back … but how are we going to move on if you'll never forgive me?"

His expression changes, and I turn around, knocking on Gia's door. She opens it seconds later, taking one look at my face, before ushering me in.

☆☆☆

He doesn't trust me. After everything we talked through, he doesn't trust me. Sure, I can understand where he's coming from, but I don't like what he was accusing me of—thinking I'd purposely withheld our marriage from Sean.

"Do you hear that?" Gia says, peeking out the window. We're sitting on opposite ends of the couch—wine in my hand, bottled water in hers. "It's raining."

"'Bout time."

She moves her hand to her belly, laughing.

"Is the baby kicking?"

She slides her hand back and forth. "No. I was just picturing Luke punching Sean. I'm bummed I missed it." When I frown, she throws a pillow at me. "You guys are gonna be fine. People do crazy things because of jealousy. Let him cool off. His head will clear by morning."

Maybe I don't want to wait 'til morning. "Do you think he has good reason to be angry? I mean, we've talked about this. He knows my relationship with Sean was because of a misunderstanding. I would never intentionally hurt him."

"You said you and Sean were hugging when he walked up?"

I nod.

"Put yourself in his position. Think of what he came back to after he left." She leans forward. "Sean rubbed your relationship in his face, stole the woman he loves. Now that he has you back, he finds you in Sean's arms again. He's not thinking rationally. Would you be?"

No, I wouldn't. "What should I do?"

"He'll come to you when he's ready." Booming thunder has me jumping, at the same time the front door swings open.

As if his ears were ringing, Luke stands at the entrance, wet from the rain. His chest is heaving. He looks unbelievably sexy, and I'm proud to know he is mine. I open my mouth then shut it, deciding not to speak.

Gia perks up with a smile. "Well, hello there, Mr. Ryann!

What brings you here on this stormy evening?"

"Came to collect my wife." His brown eyes burn into mine, as he takes confident steps in my direction. Within seconds, he swoops me up, then carries me out into the pouring rain, moving along the pathway toward our house. Once we're inside, he sets me down, his hungry gaze sweeping over me. My chest rises and falls, and I hesitantly step back.

He moves forward, a brow raised, then plants a palm on the wall behind me, challenging me. "Where you goin', sweetheart?"

"Nowhere."

His free hand slides over my bottom, caressing. "What kinda pants are these?" His voice is gravelly, his sexy mouth, distracting.

"What?"

"The pants. What are they?"

"Yoga pants."

His eyes heat, then he massages between my legs. "I love yoga pants." Shoving them over my hips, past my knees, he drops his gym shorts just as quickly. When his thumb circles my clit, I gasp. He leans forward, slipping a finger inside me, then another. My eyes roll back, and I part my lips. He pulls them out of me, showing me my arousal. "Tell me this is for me."

"It's for you," I say breathily.

He grips my hips, lifting me up, then slams into me. "I forgive you," he growls, before pounding into me relentlessly, igniting a flame that builds inside me. I moan, savoring the feeling. I've needed this—needed him to show me how much he wants me, to claim me as his. There's nothing gentle about his movements. He's rocking into me like a wild beast.

My head falls back, and I buck against him, hitting the wall behind me.

"Is this what you wanted?" he grunts.

"Yes!"

Rain drips down the side of his neck. I lean forward, licking it off him, loving the way he tastes. He fists my hair, forcing me to look at him. "Nobody touches you but me. Understand? You're mine." Pulling all the way out, he thrusts back in, his teeth clenched.

"Nobody but you."

His tongue traces my lips. He drives in deeper, continuously stroking where I need him. My entire body quakes, and I cry out his name.

"*Yes,*" he groans. "I can feel you coming." Stiffening, he pulses between my legs, drawing out his last thrust. When his body relaxes, he releases me, and my knees buckle. I slide down the wall, and he sits on the ground beside me. We're both breathing heavily.

It takes a while for either of us to speak, but eventually he looks at me apologetically. "Was I too rough?"

I turn to him. "No. I liked it … a lot actually. Nothing wrong with a little variety."

"Yeah? Want some more?" His mouth tips.

"Hmm … I'm not sure you can handle me twice in one night."

"Wouldn't be the first time."

He's right. It wouldn't.

I bite my lower lip.

"Sorry I was a dick earlier," he murmurs.

"Yeah. Me too. He was baiting you, Luke. I wanted him to leave, and he—"

Pressing his lips to mine, he says, "I believe you." Standing up, he pulls me with him. I trail behind, toward the shower. He takes off the remainder of our clothes, before we're stepping under the spray. We spend several minutes soaping each other up, kissing and touching. His fingers move between my legs. "I'm not done with you yet," he warns, his erection pointing toward me. When we're all dried off, he takes me to bed and tenderly makes love to me.

Chapter
REESE
Twenty-Eight

"We have an audience," I say to Luke, who has me pinned to the ground with a wicked grin on his face. Erica just laughs, which is what he is going for.

He rolls off me, muttering, "quitter," under his breath, before helping me up, then the three of us move toward the exit.

"I'd like to get home *some*time today. I have places to be, remember?"

"Yeah, yeah." Holding the door open, he plants a quick peck on my lips.

"You guys make a cute couple," Erica says, smiling. We thank her at the same time, and Luke winks at me.

Today was the last class of the season. I make it a tradition to show the girls how much they've grown since they'd started. Erica won Most Improved. She was shy in the beginning, eventually warming up with a strong drive to learn. We were waiting on her mother, who is over a half hour late, when Erica happened to mention the amount of time she spends at the bars, since her recent split from her boyfriend, it raised a big red flag with me.

Thankfully her mother didn't protest when I just offered to give her a ride home.

"Maybe we should steal her ... bring her home with us," I tease. "I'm gonna miss having her around."

Luke adjusts the rearview on her. "I'm cool with that. You cool with that, Erica?"

I look over my shoulder, and she's smiling. "Doubt my mom would care, or even notice. Less responsibility for her at least."

"No way! She would *totally* miss you," I scoff, feeling bad I said anything.

She looks out the window. "You don't know her like I do."

Luke and I glance at each other. I don't know what's going on in her home life, but from what she's told me, I can probably guess.

"You're planning on coming back next season, aren't you?"

"My mom isn't sure yet. I want to."

We pull into a neighborhood, getting close. I grab a pen out of my purse. "Tell you what," I say, finding a scrap of paper in the glove compartment. "I'm gonna give you my number. You ever need help—someone to talk to—call me. I don't care what time it is. Okay?" She takes the paper from me.

"Thank you."

"I mean it." I smile at her, feeling a pang in my chest. "You can call me anytime."

Luke slows to a stop in front of a small house with dark green trim. "This it?"

"Yeah." She grabs her bag. "Thanks for the ride and everything."

The concern in his eyes probably matches mine. "Anytime"

She nods then backs away, waving. Luke and I wait 'til she gets inside before we pull away.

"You okay?"

"Yeah ... I'm just ... worried about her." I blow out a long breath.

He squeezes my thigh, and I interlock our fingers. "She trusts you. She'll call you, if she needs to."

"I hope so."

Tracing small circles over my skin, he asks, "Still planning on leavin' me all by my lonesome?" He makes a sad face, one that could work on most occasions, but not today.

"I have your surprise to work on, so yes. And you won't be completely alone. You'll have Chance."

He snorts. "Definitely not the same."

"I'm sorry. I can't change my plans. They're set in stone, but it should only take an hour or so. I think you'll survive."

"I'll let you make it up to me." He moves my hand over the bulge between his legs. His lips twitch, and he adds, "Before you go."

I tighten my grip, and his eyes glaze over. "That was part of the plan."

He presses down on the gas pedal, and we pass a familiar white truck. A knot forms in the pit of my stomach. I follow it over my shoulder, spotting the metallic silver covering the windows in the back. Every time I see it, there's something unsettling that comes over me.

Luke notices my shift in mood. "What's wrong?"

I give him a reassuring smile. "Nothing."

☆☆☆

I arrive early to make sure I don't miss the delivery guys. I'm having a gym set up in one of the extra rooms. Luke's original equipment is outdated, and he's been grumbling about getting a few more weight and cardio machines. He won't accept any of my money to help out with the bills, so I figured this will be a small way to contribute. And it will allow us more time to spend at home together.

The doorbell rings, and I scurry to the entrance, facing a short, bald man, holding a yellow slip of paper. I lead him and another guy into the room, showing them where to place all the equipment. He nods and takes some measurements, estimating it to take them a couple of hours to put everything together.

I hang out in the kitchen, browsing peoples' status updates on Facebook to pass the time. I pop a cracker into my mouth, as I get an alert from the news app on my phone. I read it, sucking in a breath when I see there's been another attack, once again close to home. This time the young victim was lucky enough to get away. Apparently she had injured the suspect when trying to escape. They now have the suspect's name and have matched his DNA to some of the recent murders. My phone rings from an unknown number, pulling me away from the article, and I debate on whether to answer it.

"All set," the bald guy says, catching my attention, his partner striding out the front door with their toolbox. Turning off my ringer, I get up to meet him at the door, wiping the cracker crumbs off my fingers and onto my jeans.

I thank him and shut the door. Grabbing my stuff from the kitchen, I head to the weight room, but spot an open window on the way. *How long has this been open?* Shutting it, I lock it from the inside before another curious thought enters my mind. I quickly squash it. *There are no remnants of a squatter living here, Reese. It's probably just an accident.* I double-check the rest of the windows then finally head to weight room. We've got the cardio equipment in the back, free weights in the center, and other machines scattered about. I guzzle the rest of my water, pleased with how it turned out and reach for my phone, but it's not where I left it. *At least it's not where I thought I'd left it.* I check the kitchen and the bathroom without any luck, then tread back to the weight room. The floor creaks behind me, and I spin around, my heart nearly stopping.

"Hello?" I step toward the doorway, peeking down the hall. I swear I heard footsteps, but there's nobody there. *Maybe it was just the house settling.* There's another creak. My head snaps up, and I let out a blood-curdling scream.

"Lookin' for this?" My shattered phone rests in his hand, and all the air is sucked out of my lungs.

I back up. *No, No, No!* His dark, greasy hair is pulled back into a low ponytail. His thin lips are twisted into an evil grin, and he has that same eerie gaze that I remember from the day he nearly raped me. "Get out!" I shout, grabbing a dumbbell.

"Now, that's no way to treat a guest." His shirt is covered in blood, and his nose looks busted. He's a filthy mess. "What are you gonna do? Hit me with that?"

"I said get out!"

"Can't do that," he murmurs, stepping toward me, his eyes on my trembling hands. "Did you think I wouldn't find you? Did you think I'd forget?"

I stutter, terrified. "I think you're a twisted son of a bitch."

"Big words for such a little girl."

"Not so little anymore!" I swing the dumbbell, treading back, as he gives me a once over.

"Do you remember the last time we were together, Reese? Wrists bound behind your back. You were scared, naked."

He moves forward, and I feel a wave of dizziness, toppling over the machine behind me. He rips the dumbbell out of my hand, then slams it to the ground. I scream, crawling through the space between the machines, shuffling to stand up. My arm is yanked back. He strikes my face with the back of his other hand, then squeezes my cheeks roughly. Getting in my face, he yells, "Nobody's gonna save you this time, bitch!" He slams our mouths together, and I gag, causing him to pull back and meet his gaze. "I'm gonna tear you apart from the inside out. Then, after I *kill* you, I'll dump your defiled naked body in the desert. How's that for payback?"

"Please ... just let me go!" I whimper, feeling my limbs grow heavy.

"Sorry it has to end for you like this," he says sympathetically. "You were always a pretty thing. Weren't ya?" I ram my knee into his balls, then slam my palm into his broken nose, feeling a crack. I race to the doorway, my pulse accelerating, then am shoved forward, my face slamming down on the hardwood floor. I cry out in protest, as he wraps his arms around my knees, dragging me across the floor on my stomach. "Crazy whore," he seethes.

I look for anything I can use as a weapon, but there's nothing within my reach. My nails scrape the ground, as he climbs on top of my back. I swing back, jabbing his throat with my elbow. He makes a choking sound, flipping me over. I've never felt my heart beat so fast, but every other part of me is weakening. And my brain feels cloudy. Something is clearly wrong with me.

"You're gonna pay for that, you fuckin' slut!" He rips open my shirt. I slap at his face as he gropes my breasts, and holds me down, straddling me, his blood dripping onto my skin.

"Stop fighting!" he snarls, wrapping his hands around my neck, cutting off my air supply.

I lift my hips and push him down with my heavy limbs, gripping his face. I dig my thumbs into his eye sockets. "I'll never stop!" I scream, making his eyes bleed. He's forced to release my throat, taking my arms and stretching them above my head, as I gasp for breath.

"Feisty little bitch!"

"I won't let you win..." I slur, my head getting foggier.

"Then we'll have to wait 'til the drug kicks in. Enough of this crazy shit." He spits, watching my expression, waiting to get a reaction out of me.

Oh God. Did he really?

"That's right." He chuckles. "I drugged you. Tell me, did your water taste funny? I slipped somethin' in it when you were takin' a piss."

"You're lying!"

"Am I?"

Oh God, no! Hot tears roll down my cheeks for the innocent life living inside me—for Luke and the news I hadn't even broken to him yet. I turn away so I don't have to look at him, hating that he sees my tears, that I'm losing my strength.

"Don't *crrryyyy*. It gonna make you feel real *good*," he says, licking the tears off my cheeks. "Consider it your going away gift."

"Go to hell," I sob, as he kisses down my neck. I feel the tips of my fingers brush something behind me. He forces our mouths together, shoving his dirty tongue between my lips. Acid fills the back of my throat. I stretch my fingers, silently hoping this is God's answer to my prayers. He starts unbuttoning my jeans, and I bite down on his tongue. His coppery blood gags me, but I don't release him, and he shrieks in pain, struggling to get away from me. With my arm like deadweight, I swing my purse, smacking him in the temple.

He rolls to the side, screaming, "Fuck!" and spews a mouthful of blood.

With the effects of the drugs more potent, I fumble to find my Taser, relieved when I grab it with shaky hands. I shove it between his legs, pressing the button. A high pitch noise comes out of him. I hope his dick falls off, as I press the Taser repeatedly. I try to get up, but collapse when my legs refuse to work any longer.

Crawling on my hands and knees toward the dumbbells, I drag one over to where he lays unconscious. It takes all my strength to sit up. Using both my hands, I slam it down on his head, then do it again. The room spins, and I throw up several times, feeling my eyes grow heavy. I crawl as far away from him as I can, before everything fades into darkness.

Chapter
LUKE
Twenty-Nine

"When's your woman supposed to get here?"

I check the clock for the tenth time, then my eyes swing to Logan. "Thought she'd be home by now."

"You itchin' to go another round with her or what?"

"*That,* and she's not answering her phone." We've been watching a ball game for the last couple of hours, but I lost interest halfway through, worrying about why she wasn't home yet. She'd told me she'd only be gone an hour.

Logan adjusts his hat over his buzz cut. "Tell her what's up. The two of you got a baby to make!"

I shake my head, frustrated, and send Reese another text. I'd brought up the idea of starting a family a while back, not expecting she'd agree so easily. But she'd gotten excited about having our children grow up close in age with Logan and Gia's. She'd gone off the pill the very next day, and we've been trying ever since. "It keeps goin' directly to voicemail. Think her phone is shut off."

"That normal for her?"

"Nope."

"What time she leave?"

I rest my arms on the back of the couch, having a hard time staying still. Something doesn't feel right. "Five-thirty, six."

"Maybe her phone wasn't charged. Gia told me about your surprise. It's probably just holdin' her up. She said she's—"

"Don't tell me about it, bro. It'll piss Reese off."

"Hey," he holds out his hands, "only tryin' to help. You're being all anxious and shit."

"Am not."

"*Right*," he snorts, checking his phone. "Gia says her car's loaded with baby stuff. Guess her mom bought out the entire store."

"That kid's gonna be spoiled." They just found out they're having a boy—the first boy in Gia's family in decades. Her parents are stoked. I scratch Chance behind the ears, and he lays his head between his paws. Logan rambles on about his son, but my attention switches to the TV. They've got up an old mug shot of a person I immediately recognize. I do a double-take and lean forward. "Holy shit!" The screen switches to another familiar face, standing next to a reporter. "Dude, I know them!"

"The two chicks?"

I hold up a finger, hiking up the volume. Whatever this is, it isn't good.

The reporter begins to speak. "I'm standing here with the mother of our most recent victim, who was lucky enough to get away from the reported suspect earlier today. Her mother is reporting that the man in the picture, Ronald Cummings, jumped out of his truck, and attacked her daughter when she was walking home from a friend's house this evening. Can you explain how your daughter's quick reaction helped her escape?" The camera zooms in on Erica's mother, who's visibly shaken up, with tears in her eyes.

"He tried to pull her into his vehicle, and she fought him. She believes she broke his nose during the struggle..." She sniffs. "That's when he let her go."

"Can you tell us what he was driving?" the reporter asks.

"A white Chevy truck. The cab is extended, and the back windows are covered with foil."

The reporter repeats the description of the truck, then throws out a question that makes my blood run cold. "Now, is it true that your daughter was acquainted with this man?"

"Excuse me..." Erica's mother clears her throat, using a tissue to wipe her nose. "Ronald and I briefly dated. I wasn't aware of his criminal past until today. I'm just ... I'm just glad my baby's okay."

What are the fuckin' chances? I try Reese on her cell again, as my mind tries to piece this together. *Was he using her to get to Reese?* I stand up, looking for my keys.

"You gonna tell me why you're trippin'?"

I ignore him, slamming the drawers in the kitchen, in a panic, when I'm unable to find them.

"This report comes on the day that law enforcement held a news conference, announcing that Ronald Cummings is a prime suspect in at least *three* of the recent murders. His DNA was a match to DNA found at the crimes scenes of the female victims. They are asking that anyone who has information on his whereabouts contact law enforcement immediately."

I curse as I finally find my keys, then bolt to my closet to grab my gun. Making sure it's loaded, I stride through the house, pushing out the front door.

Logan catches up, as I head for my truck. "Where the hell you goin'?"

Clicking the alarm, I hop inside the driver seat. "What if that prick is after her?" He leans against the driver side door before I can close it.

He looks lost. "'Cause he dated the mom of a kid in your class? No offense, but ... aren't you bein' over protective? All of the victims have been younger than her."

I try to shut my door, but he doesn't budge. I don't have time to explain this shit to him. "Look, back the fuck off, or I'll lay you the fuck out."

"Dude! She bought you new gym equipment. She's havin' it delivered and set up tonight. A whole shitload of stuff!"

"That same motherfucker tried to rape Reese years ago! I stopped it from happenin' ... now get out of my way!"

"Holy shit!" His eyes widen, finally understanding. "Keep callin' her, I'll drive!" Noticing my look of protest, he adds, "You're too riled up. I'll get us there. Trust me."

Logan breaks every traffic law imaginable, while I lose my shit, unable to reach her. I slam my fist against the dashboard.

"Give your girl some credit. She's a tough chick."

"How do you expect me to react?" I bark.

"Look, I'd freak if I was in your shoes, but have a little faith. This is what you trained her for."

We roll up to the front of the house, and I cock my gun, charging out of my truck before Logan kills the engine. I push the door open and find Reese in front of the entrance. "Call an ambulance!" I yell over my shoulder, feeling for a pulse, and exhaling when I find one. She's covered in blood, her face is banged up, and her shirt is ripped down the front. Gently shaking her, I try to get her to wake up.

Her eyes stay closed, and she groans. I check to see where

the blood's coming from and soon realize it isn't hers. She had to have injured him pretty good considering the amount she's got on her clothes. She mumbles incoherently, like she's doped up.

Pulling my shirt over my head, I cover her with it. "You're safe now, baby. I'm here." I kiss her mouth, her cheeks, and her forehead, then sense Logan behind me. I turn to meet his pale face.

"Is? Is she...?" he stutters. "She isn't?"

"She's alive. I think he drugged her." I hand him my gun. "Check the rest of the house."

He cocks it then moves down the hallway.

I kiss the bruise on her cheek. "Come on, baby. Wake up." I gently cup her face, choking back my emotions, trying to stay calm for her. "*Please.* I need you to wake up." I hear her whimper, then watch her stir, before her eyes flutter open. She looks afraid and confused, taking in her surroundings. It breaks my fucking heart to see her like this. She struggles to speak, then big tears roll down her cheeks. "I'm sssorrryy," she slurs.

"Don't say you're sorry. I'm the one who's sorry — sorry I wasn't here to protect you. Sorry I didn't kill him when I had the chance." I kiss her mouth. "You're so strong, baby — so strong. I'm so proud of you." I'm not even sure if she remembers what the hell happened to her. I run my hands up and down her arms, as her teeth chatter, trying to keep her warm.

"I ... I don't knowww what's wrrroonng with me."

We need to get her to the hospital, or I'm about to freak the fuck out.

"It's okay, baby. I'm with you." I stroke her hair. "The police are on their way."

"Luke! Come here. You gotta see this," Logan shouts.

"I'm not leavin' her!" I growl. "And where the fuck is the

ambulance?"

"On their way." He strides back into the room. "Dude, you're not gonna believe this." I'm about to pound my fist into his smirking face. "She killed him ... beat the *fuuuck* out of him, man. Dude's dead. *Deader* than dead!"

My eyes fall on Reese in disbelief. "Did you do that?"

She cries weakly, her lip trembling. "Luke, I ... I'm pregnant."

☆ ☆ ☆

We'd spent several hours in the hospital that night. Right after we'd arrived, they'd taken Reese in and ran blood and urine tests, immediately confirming she was pregnant. I almost put my fist through a wall when they'd said they'd found GHB in her system. It'd taken several hours for the effects to leave her body. She was out of it, but coherent enough to worry about the drugs affecting the baby.

When they'd given Reese the ultrasound, reality had finally settled in. Seeing the flicker of our baby's tiny heartbeat had stirred something up inside me. I was going to be a daddy — the proof was right up on the screen. The nurse practitioner measured Reese to be eight weeks along, but we knew we weren't out of the woods yet. But I had to stay positive for Reese.

Officer Kerye had been nice enough to wait 'til Reese was rested before bombarding her with questions. She'd gone on and on about how brave Reese had been, calling her a hero. I'd grinned at that. My girl had outsmarted a serial killer — something the police hadn't been able to do. She'd taken the news about Erica hard, but after they'd spoken, Erica convinced her that she was okay.

Now, being in the same room where I'd found her unconscious last week, it's hard not to think about what could've happened, not to feel somewhat responsible—like I've failed her in a way, like I've failed her father and broken my promise to him.

"You have that look again," Reese says, her new confidence making her all the more tempting. She's drying her damp hair with a towel. My eyes zone in on her toned legs. She's just gotten out of the shower and is wearing the little black nighty I like. I finally meet her gaze.

"What look?"

"You know what look." She tosses the towel, striding toward me, then climbs onto my lap. Placing my hand on her belly, where our baby is growing, she says, "We're gonna be fine. I promise."

I dip my face into her neck, inhaling her scent. She smells good enough to eat. "I know, baby."

"Do you really?"

"I do."

She pulls back with a look that says she doesn't believe me, but I don't want to get into that. I've got other things on my mind—like getting her naked and wet.

Playing with the strap on her shoulder, I say, "Shame you got all cleaned up."

"Why?"

I give her a slow onceover. "Cause I feel like gettin' dirty." I rotate my hips then lean in for a kiss, but she backs away.

"Not until we talk about this. Stop trying to distract me. You've been distant lately, and I'm worried."

I notice her lip quiver. And now I realize I'm the world's biggest pussy, neglecting my pregnant wife, when she's the victim in all of this. "Sorry, baby," I sigh, kissing her forehead. "You're right." I place my hands on her hips, kiss her nose, and then her lips. "Thank you."

"For what?"

"Fightin' back."

She hops off my lap. "What can I say? I had a good teacher." She grins and unbuckles my pants, then brings them down my legs with my boxer briefs, before climbing back on top of me. She glances down at her belly. "You know ... we wouldn't have survived, if it weren't for you." I make a face, ready to tell her she did it all on her own, but she silences me with her finger. "You taught me everything I know. I think you forget that." She wraps her hand around my dick, and my breathing instantly changes.

Shoving my fingers into her hair, I bring our mouths together. Feeling her rise up on her knees, she slowly glides down on me, sinking me into her warm heat. My hips jerk up, and I groan, "You naughty, naughty girl."

She bites her lip, swinging her arms around me. I hadn't realized she wasn't wearing any panties. When I thrust my hips, I find she's soaked and ready. She lets out a quiet moan, and her eyes roll back.

Bringing the hem of her nighty up and over her head, I toss it behind me, gliding my fingers over her skin. Sitting back against the chair, I watch her ride me. And what a sight it is to see. "God, you're beautiful," I growl, kissing her pouty lips, as she circles her hips.

My mouth waters to taste her skin. I kiss her again, then drag my tongue down her neck, across her collarbone. Her head falls back, and she pushes her breasts into my face. I take advantage, greedily sucking them into my mouth. She presses closer, fisting my hair, as I lift up and drive deeper into her.

She shifts, then forces me to meet her gaze, and I swear she sees everything. "I love you," she whispers, slowly rocking against me. "So much."

I'm swelling inside her, running my palms down her back,

and guiding her with my hands. It's been awhile since I've had her. There's no way I'll last. I plunge into her harder, flexing my hips, giving it to her the way she needs it. She moans, unable to keep her eyes open. I continue to push into her, and she gasps, arching her back.

"Luke—"

Beads of sweat drip down my chest. "I love you, baby," I grunt. "You're my

everything."

Her limbs tremble. I can tell she's close. "Don't stop!"

My grip tightens on her ass, as I try not to come yet. "If I had a choice," *thrust* "I'd live," *thrust* "inside you," *thrust* "forever." I kiss her mouth, rocking into her a few more times with a groan, then we shudder together, as the sounds of our moans fill the house.

LUKE

Epilogue

"She knows her daddy," Reese says softly. "Look at the way she's watching you."

You'd never know that she'd delivered a baby a few hours ago. She still looks like an angel. I cradle my baby girl, and she gazes up at me with her almond-shaped eyes—eyes that remind me of her mother's. She's the cutest thing I've ever seen—not that I've seen a lot of newborns, but I've seen enough to know the difference. *She's special. She's mine.*

She slips her tiny thumb into her mouth, cooing. Those little noises coming out of her have my heart exploding at every beat.

"Ready to make another?" I'm mostly serious. I'd have a dozen more if Reese wanted.

"Ask me later." She cringes, scooting up on the bed. "My vagina needs a break."

"Not too long of a break I hope."

I grin down at Story, as she makes another noise. "She says she wants a brother." Her face turns a deep shade of red, then she kicks out her feet. A sound I've never heard from a girl comes out of her tiny body, then she whimpers like it scared her. "Think she filled her diaper."

"I wish I had a camera. You should see your face right now," Reese giggles.

Story's cries get louder, so I stand up and rock her.

"Here, I'll give you back to Mommy. She's knows what to do."

Reese shakes her head when I try to hand her over. "Oh no, you don't. You're going to be a diaper-changing machine by the time we get out of here. Plus, I really want to watch you change your first poopy diaper." She combs her fingers through her hair, a wide smile on her face. She thinks this is funny.

"I've changed a diaper once or twice," Of course, *that was over twenty years ago.*

She arches a brow, disbelieving. "When? Whose?"

"Ask my sister when she comes. She'll tell you."

"*Okay*, show me your skills then. Let's see if you remember."

"Hear that, baby girl? Your momma thinks I don't know how to change a diaper. But you have faith in Daddy, don't ya?"

Her mouth makes a little O.

"Yeah? Glad somebody does." I carry Story over to the changing table that I'd seen the nurse use earlier, right as Logan and Gia walk back into the room.

"Now that's adorable," Gia says.

"How's the hospital food?"

"Sucks," he grumbles.

"I agree," Reese replies, her eyes still fixed on our baby.

Logan waves a hand. "Dude, I can smell that shit from here. Hurry and change her. Will ya?"

"Give my daughter some privacy." I snort. "Besides, I've smelled much worse outta Jax." I peel off her dirty diaper.

"Speaking of Jax," Gia chimes in. "We have to leave."

"Who's watching him?" Reese asks.

"My mom. She says he's being fussy—poor little man. We think he might be teething." She turns her attention back to Story. "I wanna hold her again, though, before we leave. She really is a beautiful baby, guys. Good work."

"Takes after her mom." I smirk.

Logan chuckles. "Just wait, bro. You're gonna need to get out a shotgun when the boys come a'knockin'."

"Oh, *stop it*. Jaxon will keep the boys away," Gia murmurs.

My eyes swing from her to Logan. "That supposed to make me feel better?"

"What, dude? My son's a stud."

"You were every father's worst nightmare." I toss the soiled diaper in the trash.

"Nah, Jax and Story will be friends." He shrugs. "He'll look after her and shit."

"Exactly. And shit," I grunt, feelin' extra protective of my daughter.

"Hey, at least you know the parents, if they end up together."

I lift my daughter, proudly admiring my work. "Not so bad. Is it?"

"Wow." Reese smiles. "I'm impressed."

I stride toward Gia, then hand over a swaddled Story. She and Logan take turns holding her, before they say their goodbyes.

"Can you believe this little person is a part of us?" Reese asks, lying on her side, facing me, Story nestled between us.

"She's perfect." My gaze switches back and forth between them. Never believed I'd be blessed enough to actually have a family, but they're here, and it's the best feeling in the world.

"What are you thinking?" she asks quietly.

"'Bout how lucky I am." I carefully lean over and kiss her forehead, then lean down and kiss the back of one of Story's little hands.

Reese's face warms, then her brows bunch together. "Do you think I can be a good mother?"

Reaching over, I stroke her cheek. "You're gonna be an amazing mother. I'm proud of you, baby. I have no doubts you'll be great."

"I'm proud of you, too. You're already a great father. You're sweet with her ... I think it's kind of adorable."

I hope she's right. "Didn't have much of a teacher. God knows I'm gonna fail sometimes," I say, swallowing. "I'm gonna do whatever it takes to protect my girls. I'm confident in that at least."

She glances at Story. "I'm glad she already has a little friend to play with."

My mood darkens, and a low growl comes out of me.

She frowns. "What's that for?"

I look at our sleeping daughter. "Wondering if we made the right decision."

"About what?"

"Logan and Gia ... livin' next door to us."

She rises up on her elbow, with her eyebrows peaked. "You're serious?"

I nod, and she narrows her eyes on me.

"You're worried about Story and Jax?" She's biting back a laugh.

"Laugh now, but if he's anything like his father, we're gonna have a serious problem. I grew up with the guy."

"*Oh boy...*" She looks down at Story, gently rubbing her soft, fuzzy head. "I already feel sorry for you, baby."

"It's my job as a father to protect her."

"And you will."

"Damn right I will." *This isn't a joke. I'm fuckin' serious.*

"You *do* realize they're just babies," she says, before she kisses me. "Relax. We don't have to worry about this for a long time. Okay, Mr. Protective?" She's right. I calm myself. I guess it is a little early for me to worry about this. "Let's cross that bridge once we get there. For now, let's enjoy our brand new baby girl."

I exhale a breath, and kiss my daughter on top of her head.

Then, that's just what we do. We lie there, and we enjoy our baby girl.

THE END

Thank you for reading the Bad Boy Reformed Series! Join my email list, and checkout my Facebook page, to stay posted on Story and Jax's story, as well as my future books.

Acknowledgments

Gosh! There are so many people to thank. If I leave anybody out, please don't be offended, and know that it isn't on purpose. First and foremost, thank you to God for blessing me with so much more than I deserve. To my *'Darling Dolls.'* Thank you for your consistent loyalty, and for believing in me from the very beginning. I love you all dearly! Thank you to my family for putting up with my absence on many occasions, so that I could finish the series. Thank you to my husband for taking care of our children while I was zoned out on the computer for several hours at a time. Thank you to Camryn and Rachelle for critiquing each chapter of Breaking Ryann, and giving me your input. To Alex Michael Turner for allowing me to use you for my beautiful cover photos. I'm sure my readers thank you too. To Madison Seidler for editing my mistakes, and to Sarah Hansen for your wonderful cover art. To Emily Tippetts, for making the pages of my story pretty. A special thanks to *all* of you bloggers who have taken the time to read, review, and spread the word about my books- Please know that I appreciate you for all that you do. To Brandi, Lynn, Amy, Cris, Kerye, and several others- I SEE YOU. Thank you so much for putting my teasers out there, and for being the selfless women that you are. I can't express how grateful I am to have your support and friendship. Last but not least- thank you to every single reader for taking a chance on my stories, and thank you all for your patience with me on completing the series.

About the Author

Wife. Mother. Writer. Reader. Dreamer.

For more information on Alyssa Rae Taylor and her up and coming projects, you can visit her here:

https://www.facebook.com/authoralyssaraetaylor
https://www.goodreads.com/alyssaraetaylor
https://twitter.com/Alyssartaylor
https://www.alyssaraetaylor.com

Made in the USA
Middletown, DE
05 October 2015